JESSICA CRANBERRY

A HORDE OF DEAD POETS

A BETTER GRAVE THAN THIS

JESSICA CRANBERRY

Percy's Heart Press www.percysheartpress.com

Book Layout

Edited by Carla Lewis, Jess Moore

Cover Art and Design © 2024 Adina Chiles

Interior Formatting by Book Savvy Services

Credit to: Wylie, Elinor. "Epitaph", *Black Armour*, 1923

Content Warning; Depictions of Suicide.

For this she starred her eyes with salt
And scooped her temples thin,
Until her face shone pure of fault
From the forehead to the chin.

In coldest crucibles of pain
Her shrinking flesh was fired
And smoothed into a finer grain
To make it more desired.

Pain left her lips more clear than glass;
It colored and cooled her hand.
She lay a field of scented grass
Yielded as pasture land.

For this her loveliness was curved
And carved as silver is:
For this she was brave: but she deserved
A better grave than this.

Elinor Wylie
"Epitaph"

Contents

One

Truly Butcher was nobody's bitch. Loud? Sure. Obnoxious? Absolutely. Lazy? Uh-huh. But nobody, *nobody*, took advantage of Truly Butcher. So that's why she had been, and continued to be, so pissed about her piece of shit boyfriend of the last three years cheating on her for over half of that time. She cranked the car stereo, and scream-sang Miley Cyrus's "Wrecking Ball" as she sped down route 27. Back to Moss Landing. Back to where she came from.

The song ended and some RV salesman took over the radio waves. Truly stabbed the power button and grabbed her purse. She pulled out a pack of cigarettes and ripped the cellophane off with her teeth. She lit up and took a long drag, sure as hell whatever burned inside damaged her lungs. Though Truly wasn't a long-term smoker, only when the shit hit the fan. And that it did, often enough. She knew cancer would get her in the end, no matter what.

Ever'body gotta die some kinda way, her grammaw used to say.

And when generations of family spent their whole lives living next to a condemned nuclear processing plant, it was gonna be some kind of cancer-way. Every tenth house in Moss Landing someone died from the Big C. It had been true for Grammaw as well—stomach, guts rotted through to the core. Everyone knew the uranium dust that had been spewed into the atmosphere and now layered throughout the soil and water had done it, but what were a bunch of hillbillies gonna do? They had mortgages to pay and children to feed, certainly not the money it would take to prove a damn government-funded causality.

Truly dropped the last of her cigarette, *tzzz,* into the little bit of soda left in her Big Gulp. She sailed past the Moss Landing exit—now boasting two different Cincinnati chili places and a brand-new Taco Bell—toward the turn off where her childhood home sat tucked among a grove of ash trees.

Gravel popped under her tires as she rode up the long driveway. The house wasn't much to brag about—old and saggy siding, paint peeling in spots—but it had been home to several generations of Butcher women. And for Truly, it was a place of refuge, a place to go when everything had gone sideways, and all plans had failed. At least, it had been when Grammaw was alive. Now, Truly would be rooming with just her mother and that relationship was...complicated.

Truly parked and looked around before getting out of her car. She was back. Again. Dumped by some loser her mom had warned her about. Another cheater. Another asshole who wasn't worth the toilet paper she wiped her ass with.

Truly got out of the car and walked toward the house, the spongey, wet green of Southeastern Ohio this time of year, springing her feet forward. Elsewhere they called this time of day golden hour, but in these parts of the surrounding woods, the light always stayed a kind of gray-green. Calmness seeped through her skin. Her jaw unclenched, and she lowered her shoulders. No matter what, this was home, and a deep, bone-setting nostalgia did something to the back of her brain.

A bright red cardinal flitted among the branches encroaching the roof, and Truly thought spotting one might mean good luck. But then she noted all the spindly bareness, an anomaly this time of year. A lot of the trees in the area were dead or dying—had been for years now. Mourning woods, she called it. The larvae of the emerald ash borer ate them alive. Squirmy little fuckers would feed until they all died.

Her mom could've treated the trees, soil drenched the base with insecticide, but they'd already been told by every news outlet it was practically hopeless. The trees would die no matter what they tried, and if cancer didn't kill her mother, these might fall over and crush the house with her and Truly in it. Neither of them had any interest in calling a specialist to bring them down though. It would feel too much like they were desecrating graves. Let the mourning woods mourn, she thought.

As Truly made her way up the rickety front porch, she chose her steps carefully, because it sure as hell didn't seem like the rotting planks could support weight. The smell of browning hamburger wafted through the screen door, along with the chirpy delivery of the evening news.

Truly didn't bother knocking. She stepped inside and let the screen door slam behind her.

"Mom!" she called.

Beyond the living room, a shadow moved in the kitchen. The metallic clank of pots and pans rang out. A wooden spoon clattered against the counter. Her mother cooked like a maniac, even when it was just those boxed meals with the cartoon glove mascot.

Truly grabbed the remote off the arm of the worn sofa, noting her mother's indentations in the cushions, and turned the TV off. She set her backpack near the hall that led upstairs to her old bedroom and walked toward the kitchen.

Her mother had a stereo going too, playing 1950s oldies, early doo-wap shit. Truly watched as her mother twirled and spun across the linoleum: stirring, tearing open the spice packet, dumping it in a pot and then winging it toward the trash can, little specks of who knew what sprinkling along the floor.

"Hey, Mom." Truly knew how her mother would react —the absolute drama of being interrupted—but also, she knew there was no way to avoid the spectacle, no matter how she greeted her mother.

"Oh! Sweet Jesus!" Her mom jumped like Truly knew she would. The spoon flew from her hand and landed with a *schmuck* on the counter. "Truly, honey, you scared the crap out of me! Living alone in these woods, I just don't have company." She clutched at where her heart should be.

"Mom, I called."

"Yes, but I didn't know *when* you'd be here!"

But Truly noticed the extra food she'd made and the table set for two. This was all part of one of her mother's performances, and Truly just went with it because why argue over something so stupid, so inconsequential. If her mother wanted to pretend to be frightened, well, who cared? The woman was probably pretty bored, living alone out here in the middle of nowhere.

What Truly couldn't ignore though, what stabbed her in the heart every time, was the look on her mother's face when she first glimpsed Truly. It was only a nano-second, a mere flicker behind the eyes, but it was there. And it was disgust.

Her mother hated hated hated Truly's body. It had started around puberty, when Truly's hips and ass grew wide. At least that's when Truly pinpointed it and started understanding that her own mother didn't approve of the way she looked, was embarrassed by her. But maybe it had been there from birth. Maybe she hated Truly's body for hijacking her own; who knew after this many years?

"Look at you!" her mother said, holding out her arms for a hug. "You've lost weight!"

"No, I haven't." Truly moved forward and hugged her mother, feeling how fragile, how insubstantial her skin and bones felt beneath her palms. "You have though." Truly regretted the words as soon as they moved past her lips. Her mother could live for weeks on those words alone. She was tiny, nothing more than a pine needle, and she employed all manner of *trends* to keep herself that way, including barely eating and chain smoking.

"Oh no! I'm as fat as ever." But the only thing anyone could have pinched on her was a tad bit of loose and wrinkling neck skin. "Dinner is almost done! And then we can sit and catch up."

"Do you need any help?" Truly asked, hoping she could just sit down.

"No, sit. Pour yourself some tea. Or wine. Whatever you want."

Truly chose the tea, not wanting to get tipsy with her

mother and say a bunch of shit she really meant. Eloise, Elly for short, completed her little cooking dance and presented Truly with a plate of glorified slop and a side salad of chopped iceberg lettuce. Truly took the plate, resignation over the whole scenario settling over her, and her mom chattered on about whatever town gossip she had fresh in her memory.

"You remember Tamara Faye, from down the road?"

Truly nodded. Of course she did. The Fayes had lived "down the road" her whole life. They were a burly bunch, prone to loud summer parties that ended with shotguns being fired into the canopy.

"Her son Brad—he went to school with you, didn't he—well, the FBI showed up here looking for him."

"The FBI? What for?"

Elly puckered her lips as if she'd just popped a lemon slice in her mouth. "Some *unsavory* pictures on his computer."

"If it was the FBI, then you mean like, kiddie porn. Jesus, Mom."

"Tamara marched right over here and told me he would never do such a thing, but he's gone. Nobody can find him."

"That's..." But Truly didn't know how to finish the sentence. It was disgusting to think someone she'd grown up with was straight up evil, but then was it really all that surprising? Brad had always been a fucking creep. When he'd shown up at high school parties, every girl knew to never be alone with him and never accept a drink from him. They'd joke about him being such a loser. But all along, real danger, real malice, had been right there. And they had just laughed.

"Horrible, Mom. That's really disgusting." Truly poked a fork into the mushy noodle mix on her plate.

"And Susan Parrish, one of my oldest friends. She owns the greenhouse down the way, remember?"

"Of course I do. She's basically family." Truly liked Susan and never really understood why someone so cool liked hanging out with her mother, but they'd grown up together.

"Cancer."

Truly blew out a breath, then scooped more casserole into her mouth and chewed, even though she barely needed to. She could have just pressed the mush up against the roof of her mouth and swallowed. This is what coming home was always like, a constant doomscroll. Only instead of the news feeling distant and nebulous, it came for people Truly was actually familiar with and cared about. It left her feeling hollow and powerless.

"What kind?" Truly asked.

"Pancreatic." Elly's mouth formed a straight line. Everyone they'd known with pancreatic cancer had been a goner, and quickly.

"Is there anything good happening?" Truly asked, ignoring how her mother hadn't eaten anything.

Elly brightened, puffing a constant stream of cigarettes. She was well into her second glass of wine. "Well, yeah! Did ya see we got a Taco Bell?"

"Yeah, Mom. I saw it when I drove past the exit."

"You wouldn't even recognize downtown!"

Truly licked a speck of creamy hamburger off her back molar. Downtown hadn't ever been more than a strip of road that led to the high school, pig farms, and that defunct nuclear processing plant. They'd had a single pizza joint, a grocery store, and an antique "mall" but times, they were a'changing, even in Moss Landing.

"There's a flea market tomorrow. Wanna go?" Elly asked.

"Sure," Truly agreed. What else was she going to do? She scooped the last of her dinner into her mouth and offered to clean up.

"Are you gonna tell me what happened this time?" Elly asked.

Truly set her plate in the sink with a heavy *clink*. Her shoulders sagged. "It just didn't work out, Mom."

"Never does with you." Elly paused, took a long drag off her cigarette, then added, "I don't know why you think you'll ever keep a man, looking like ya do."

"There it is."

Her mother's words acted like a sugar spoon, scooping out tiny pieces of Truly's heart, her confidence, herself. Truly gripped the counter, gritting her teeth. Her mother's disdain wasn't usually vocalized until glass three of wine, but when she turned, she saw Elly pouring herself that third glass.

"Oh, don't look at me like that." Elly rolled her eyes. "I'm just being honest. That Phil was an asshole."

"I won't disagree with you about him."

"At the same time, it wouldn't kill ya to lose a little weight."

"And it wouldn't kill you to lay off the wine." Truly swiped the bottle from the table and headed out the back door.

"Hey! Bring that back!"

Outside, on the back porch, Truly heard her mom's chair scrape against the linoleum. She swigged from the bottle. The too-sweet punch on her tongue left her wanting nothing but water.

"Where do you think you're going?" Her mother's silhouette filled the screen door. Such a tiny fragile thing she was, who wielded way too much power over Truly.

"Just getting the hell away from you, Mom," Truly mumbled and turned away from her mother. She pounded down the porch steps that led to an overgrown garden and shed, then beyond to a trail into the woods.

"Don't be so sensitive," her mother growled. With the *click* of a lighter and the whoosh of her mom's breath of smoke, like some sentinel gust of wind, Truly was pushed further away.

She'd given up on the two of them having a *Gilmore Girls*-esque mother/daughter relationship a long-ass time ago. Still, Truly headed for the woods to clear her head. She hated being in the position of needing something from Elly. But what were her choices? She'd sold off her belongings and moved in with Phil early in their relationship. She had nothing now. He'd told her to quit her job and stay home to take care of the house, which she'd happily done, only to find out her cleaning was never good enough and her cooking was subpar. He asked her to change her hair color to blond and she'd obliged, the too-light strands falling in her eyes as she marched through the woods. She had to face it—she'd absolutely been his bitch. Phil had spotted her as an easy mark because that's exactly what she was. Truly wasn't as strong as she liked to think herself to be. Not as burly or non-conforming. She'd turned into an easy-bake Suzy Bundtcake without even questioning it.

When Truly stopped walking and looked up at the sky, evening had begun to fall in earnest and darkness spread under the canopy. Lightning bugs flickered all around, twinkling lights flashing green and yellow.

The mourning woods had always been a sanctuary for Truly, always been a place to get away from her mother, so she wasn't worried about getting lost. She could sleepwalk her way back, the muscle memory of those steps still strong. She let herself sink to the ground, and leaned against a tree trunk to watch the fireflies do their thing. She put her hands in the pockets of her hoodie and her fingers hit something slim and hard.

Yes! She pulled out her vape, set the mouthpiece on her lips and pressed the power button, hoping it was charged, hoping it had enough of something in there for one hit. It did. She inhaled, held her breath a few seconds, then blew it out. Just the ritual of the act brought calm.

She set her gaze toward the higher tree limbs and glimpsed the first twinkle of stars, knowing instinctively where they'd show up in the sky this time of year.

Home, somehow, felt both familiar and strange at the same time.

The black of night began to crowd her, and goosebumps broke out along her arms. Something, she couldn't put her finger on exactly what, felt unsafe. A twinge in the air, some bit of electricity or pheromone. The wanted neighbor could be out here, watching her, and her breath hitched in her throat at the thought. She poured out the rest of the wine, upturning the bottle. It would make a weapon if needed. It wasn't nothing.

The moss on which she sat began to glow a deep shade of teal, a darker, cooler shade than the lightning bugs. A tendril of what she thought might be a fern, hoped and begged was a fern, tickled her wrist.

"Fuck this," she spat the word and scrambled to a standing position. She shook her head, disbelieving what she'd felt, determined to stop scaring herself. Marching back toward her mother's house, she ditched her weed pen in the yard waste bin near the shed, then looked back at the forest.

The glow remained.

Two

MOSS LANDING, 1943

Paulette "Paulie" Duhn was what the old folks around Moss Landing liked to call a "firecracker." She figured they referred to her in such a way 'cause she was big and loud and annoying to them most of the time.

It 'bout killed Paulie to sit still each morning while Ms. Jones talked letter sounds and sums and geography. Every day she'd perch on the edge of her wooden seat, waiting for that big bell out front of the schoolhouse to clang, so she could move freely in the wide, open world.

Today would be different though. She and Beau Butcher, who'd been makin' eyes at her all morning, had been going off to the little pond behind the schoolhouse at lunch break for weeks. There'd be no kissin' this afternoon. She wouldn't let him set a finger on her, even though his touch 'bout set that good kind of fire throughout her body every time. No, not today. Because today she had to tell Beau Butcher he was 'bout to be a daddy.

Clang-clang-clang. The school bell rang and everyone stood to leave. The little kids made a beeline for the door, never forgetting their lunches their mamas packed carefully for them, even if it was just a piece of bread or a half-wrinkled apple from the cellar. None of them would ever forget how hungry they used to be, that great gnawing right at the center of a body, as if there were some kind of hole that needed fill-in'; it would never go away—scarcity always being right around the corner.

Paulie felt a buzzing unpleasantness in her chest, nerves, her mama called it. Beau crossed the school room and made his way toward her. A mischievous twinkle in his blue-green eyes. He had black hair that he kept long on top, so it tended to fall perfectly around his face. He pushed it back constantly, and it just kept fallin' right back. A beautiful dance, Paulie thought.

"You wanna go have lunch together?" he asked.

"You already know I do, Beau Butcher." She liked to call him by his full name, loved the way it felt in her mouth and the rhythmic way it hit her ears. She hoped after she told him 'bout the baby, sometime soon his name would be part of hers.

They walked together outside, him not taking her hand until they were well out of view of Ms. Jones. Weeds grew tall out back, 'cept for the little trail of folded and stomped over grass that led to the pond. The older kids had a spot back here where they liked to eat, throw rocks in the water, and complain about their lessons and their lives, all the work that needed doin' once they got home. They didn't have much time to be idle, in fact these twenty minutes for lunch were 'bout it.

Beau led Paulie past the group; Nancy Ross lookin' scan-dalized the whole time. She donned the same pinched mouth and raised eyebrows she'd had since the first time Beau asked

Paulie to walk with him 'round the other side of the pond. Well, Paulie didn't care. She wanted this time with Beau as much as he did. It was a kind of fun nobody'd ever told her 'bout. They'd only warned her how bad it was, how it would hurt. But that was only true that first time, and the fire that built up inside her when Beau slid his thumb over certain spots she hadn't even known about, well, that was worth any bit of pain. She loved him for that fire. And while she trailed behind him, she worried what he might say—how all this could go away. Maybe Beau didn't want to have a family yet, maybe he had bigger plans. Maybe he'd take his magic fire fingers and use 'em on some other girl, and she'd be left alone with a screaming, crying baby. Either way, everything was bound to change.

When they reached their usual corner, he turned to her, pulling her close. "You okay?"

She nodded, the inside of her mouth suddenly as dry and tough as jerky.

"Come on, don't lie to me." He pressed his lips to her forehead, and she wrapped her arms around his waist. She breathed in his smell, like a freshly toiled garden, one last time before she altered their lives forever.

"Beau Butcher, we made us a baby." Hugged against him, she wasn't sure he heard her until he stopped massaging her back. His whole body stiffened. Oh he'd heard. She tilted her head, chin resting on his firm chest, and watched his jaw clench. "Well? What do we do now?"

"Guess we better ask your daddy if you can marry me."

A flood of feeling rushed through Paulie. She could've jumped up and down, but she was afraid she would've floated off into the blue sky, so she held on to Beau instead.

"We don't need to ask my daddy nothin'. I can marry you if I want. And I say yes."

He laughed at that. "It's proper. And state law, I think."

"To hell with proper and law. Let's go tell the preacher now. He'd do it, I bet."

Beau smoothed Paulie's hair back from her face. "No, we done some part of this backward already. So we're gonna do it right, okay?"

Paulie bit her lip but couldn't hold back her smile. "Okay," she agreed.

"You're gonna be my wife, Paulette Duhn, even if they ship me off to Europe next spring?"

"Butcher. Paulie Butcher. Sounds almost as good as yours."

He kissed her then, long and deep. Somewhere in the distance the school bell rang again, warning that their time together was almost over.

Three

Truly woke in her childhood room. The wallpaper, with its Southwestern-ish design, peeled away from the wall in spots. Blue-green light filtered its way through the tree canopy, casting the room in cool tones. There was still enough ash trees left alive to provide that comfort.

She smelled coffee, which was always good. Truly rolled out of bed and pulled on a pair of leggings and an extra-large cardigan sweater that belted around her waist like a robe. *The better to hide yourself with,* her thoughts mimicking her mother's voice. She tied her hair into a messy bun and started downstairs.

In the stairwell, she stopped and looked at all the old pictures, letting her fingers trace the frame of her grandmother's, Wilamena, Willy for short. She'd been a firecracker of a person, always booming with laughter, always snarky as hell, just like her great-grandmother, Paulie, folks who knew them both had said. It always made Truly wonder where the hell Ellie came from. The woman had no sense of humor and cared way too much about what other people thought.

Ellie told a different story about her mother. She insisted Willy hadn't been that fun-loving, happy-go-lucky, boisterous woman within the walls of their home. Willy's mother, Paulie, had lived through the Depression, so she'd spent her childhood counting every can in the cupboard, analyzing every kernel and bean that passed through the family's bowels. Only to die by suicide when Willy was little. Plus WW II had left Willy fatherless. Trauma with a capital T had clawed its way through time and made its presence palpable in Elly's childhood.

Then there'd been Willy's obsession over the possibility that Moss Landing had its very own serial killer. Ellie described the mother from her formative years as sitting at the kitchen table poring over old newspapers and searching through missing person ads. Willy had put together throughlines no police detective ever believed. On bad nights, she'd turn to drink and tell all her crazy theories as if they were bedtime stories. On good nights, a warning was never far from Willy's lips. Hyper-vigilant, they might call it now. Elly spoke of endless rules and limits about where she could venture off to. At a young age, Elly knew her mother's patterns of behavior, could recognize the moments before Willy's mood darkened, and spent hours hiding until everything went quiet. Age had mellowed Willy though, and Truly never witnessed that side of her grammaw, but she experienced the mark it had left on her mother.

"What the hell are you doing lurking like that?"

Truly startled. "Jesus, Mom. You scared me."

"Well you scared me, looking like a creep hanging out in the stairwell."

"I was just looking at these old pictures."

"The past is dead. Come down from there. Coffee's made."

Truly noticed she didn't say anything about breakfast. And sure enough, nothing had been set out to eat except for a bowl of apples on the table. *Subtle.* Truly refused to pick one up and eat it on principle. She poured herself some coffee instead, leaving the skim milk out of it—why bother—then joined her mother in the living room.

Elly sat in her rocking chair next to the front windows she propped open every morning no matter the temperature. The birds held a riot outside, chirping and flitting around the feeders Elly hung off the front porch. She motioned to the chair across from hers and Truly sat.

She tried not to be obvious about staring at her mother. But mentally Truly took inventory, noting the way Elly's breath wheezed a little at the end of each inhale, and how her shoulders sloped forward. The crook in her back was more pronounced than last time Truly had seen her and her hair, which had always been thin, no longer covered parts of her scalp.

"Awful, isn't it?" Her mother rasped.

"What?"

"Aging. It's god damned degrading to end up looking like this." Her lips flattened. "Like a witch in the woods."

"Mom...you look fine," Truly said. "But also, who cares?"

"Everyone cares, Trulia Jane. Haven't I taught you a damn thing about how the world works?"

Truly gulped her too hot coffee, letting the burn rest on her tongue before swallowing. How could she stay here? Elly was miserable and would drag Truly down with her before too long. But Truly didn't have much money. And she didn't have a job. So down to the wallowing depths with her mother she would go.

"You said there was a flea market today?"

Elly nodded. "Doesn't open till nine though. I wanna be the first ones there. It's the only way to get anything good."

"Where's it at?"

"The Grove. Where else would it be?"

Truly ignored her mother's snark. "You want me to drive?"

"That'd be nice. Since you're not paying rent."

"I will pay you as soon as I get a job."

"Not much opportunity 'round here for that."

Truly sucked a breath deep into her lungs and held it for a beat. "Okay, then. I'm gonna brush my teeth, splash some water on my face..." She stood to leave. "Slit my wrists."

"What's that?"

"Nothing. I'll be ready in a sec."

In her room, she grabbed her toothbrush from her bag, cursing herself for not remembering toothpaste—another thing she'd need to borrow from her mom. She went to the hall bath, closed the door and sighed, staring at herself in the mirror of the medicine cabinet. Her mother was wrong about Truly's appearance. She may not have stood out in a room, but she wasn't a complete slob either. Was she bigger than most women? Yeah, but not just in weight. She was nearly six feet tall. And she'd never felt the need to apologize for her size unless she was with her mother.

She really did splash water on her face, even though she felt like a TV cliché. She opened the medicine cabinet and grabbed the tube of toothpaste. As she squeezed some out onto the bristles of her brush, she took in the teal green sparkle of it and remembered the glow from last night.

It couldn't have been real. The twinkle and glow of the lightning bugs must've played tricks on her eyes. And the long drive up from Kentucky must've worn her out. That had to be it. But then...she *had* felt as if someone was watching her. Had that been her mind playing tricks too? Certainly. One hundred percent. Except what had Elly said about the neighbor? He was missing. On the run. Could he have been out there prowling about, spying on her?

Truly had lived long enough to understand some guys liked to scare women, but she shook the thought away. No. There'd been no glow on the ground. No shadowy figure watching her. She was just feeling paranoid about being back here. She started brushing her teeth and gagged as the toothbrush scraped over that one spot on the back of her tongue.

"Truly! Let's go already!"

"Coming, Mom!" Truly pinched the apples of her cheeks like an old Hollywood starlet, and whispered, "It's temporary. Living with her is a pit stop. That's it. You can do this." She blew out one more deep breath, then left the woodsy-cinnamon potpourri smell of the bathroom behind her.

ELLY SAT ON THE COUCH WITH HER COAT ON, remote in hand, fast forwarding through a commercial.

"I thought you said you were ready," Truly said, as she reached the bottom of the stairs.

"I am. Just wanna see who was eliminated last night."

"Eliminated? What are you watching?"

"*The Beholder's Eye.*"

"That plastic surgery show? I thought that went off the air years ago."

"Just changed networks. Shhh!"

On the screen a bruised and battered woman appeared. She spoke as if drunk, slurring her words yet admitting this would all be worth it in the end. Music swelled and the screen blurred through a transition.

"Linda, come on down!" the host yelled, sounding as if Linda were just a contestant on *The Price is Right*. The camera panned to a set of pink, glittery drapes. After a beat, the curtains slowly parted to reveal Linda, the woman who could barely speak mere moments ago, looking flawless. Makeup contoured her cheeks, and the perfect glint of white light highlighted the tip of her brand-new button nose. The screen split to show a stunning before-and-after shot.

Truly's mother gasped. "She looks amazing!"

"She looks traumatized," Truly mumbled, although that wasn't necessarily true. Truly was just projecting. Linda looked happy, proud even. She blotted away tears as the host talked her through how shitty she'd felt about herself in the before picture. How the woman she used to be was a stranger to her now that she'd been given the opportunity to be on the show.

"And if you make it to the next round?" the host asked.

Linda stuttered. "Oh, I-I don't know. I've always been so focused on my nose; I haven't really considered what to do next."

Come on, Linda. They're not just gonna give someone a free nose job and send them on their way. The stakes had to rise, or it wouldn't be a show.

"Lips, tits, ass, baby!" The host swung his arm behind him, moving as if to slap Linda's bottom, but he refrained at the last second. He stood next to her, swinging his arm like some kind of performing monkey. "That's the point of the game, dear."

"Well, maybe I wouldn't mind if my breasts were higher?"

"Ah, yes! Are they flopping like pancakes these days?"

The audience roared with laughter. Linda froze under the lights. Truly gaped at the screen. The FCC got their panties in a bunch over a stray f-word, but not a show hacking away at women's bodies for entertainment?

"Mom, come on. Let's go."

"Be quiet!" Elly waved a hand in Truly's direction. "Susan will already know who's been eliminated and I don't want it spoiled when we get to the market."

"Fine," Truly sat and tried to ignore the mesmerizing aspects of the show. It drew her in with ugly duckling sob stories and bullying. Who could deny the lure of that trope?

She drew the line at the surgery scenes though, watching someone's whole face being peeled off didn't sit well with Truly. She pulled out her phone and mindlessly scrolled through one of her social media feeds. Giving something a heart every once and awhile, but mostly the internet had gone stale. Just endless noise, people making the same joke over and over, or sharing whatever shitty opinion popped into their head and labeling it a hot take for likes. Everything else was just ads.

Truly's gaze moved back to the TV screen as the host called contestants up to the platform. Each one received a necklace, a choker made of black satin ribbon. As the host clasped one of the necklaces around Linda's neck, a silver charm in the shape of a swan dangled at the woman's clavicle. It's ruby eye glinted under the show's spotlights.

When the show devolved into a woman named Gloria

crumpling to the ground and weeping after not receiving a necklace of her own, Elly pressed the pause button and turned off the TV.

"I knew it would be Gloria."

"How? What criteria are they using to cut them?" Truly flinched. "I mean, from the show. How do they figure who leaves?"

"Audience vote."

"Really?"

"Yeah, Susan and I call in every week and place our votes on who we think should stay."

"Mom, this is weird."

"Not any weirder than all that trash on your Ticky-Tocky." Elly struggled a bit to lift herself off the couch. "Ready?"

"Yes. Remember you yelled at me to hurry up?"

"*Pfft*, stop being so whiny. Is that what you're wearing?"

Truly looked down at her oversized sweater and leggings. "To a flea market? Yes."

Elly raised her eyebrows in disapproval. The old woman wore a pair of jeans and a white oxford shirt. She'd done her hair and makeup. But this was literally just a flea market, so Truly refused to change.

"Come on, Mom." *Let's get this over with.*

Elly left her mug on the coffee table and grabbed her purse. Truly walked outside and waited on the front porch while her mother locked up. A dozen different shades of green dotted the forest undergrowth. It was lush and thicker than she'd ever seen it, difficult to plod through. The barren ash trees allowed more sunlight down here, so the understory had flourished.

In the distance, Truly caught a glimpse of that sparkling teal light she'd seen the night before.

"Mom, have you noticed—"

"How big your ass looks in that outfit? Yes, yes I have."

Truly bit her lower lip, restraining the urge to haul off and swing at the woman. "Better to have an ass than just bones, Mom."

"Nothing looks as good as skinny feels." Elly huffed and threw her keys in her purse.

"Tastes, Mom. Nothing *tastes* as—never mind."

"You're still driving that old clunker?"

"It works fine. Why get rid of it?"

"It's old."

"Well, so are you." Truly laughed.

"Wh—how dare—"

"Oh, don't look so scandalized. I'm just joking with you. I'm not quite ready to haul you off to the landfill."

Elly swallowed her indignation and got into the car. Truly hoped she'd get the silent treatment for the rest of the morning. She opened the driver-side door and scooted in next to her mother.

"Keep making comments about my ass though and we'll see."

Four

MOSS LANDING, 1948

"Paulie! Beau-baby! You made it!" Beau's mother, Mildred, embraced her son amid the crowd of people mingling around her patio. Mil and Bob's annual Fourth of July parties were always rumored to be epic, but Paulie never knew how much so as her family had never been invited before she and Beau were wed. This year was even bigger since they'd put in their own swimming pool, an extravagance most families in Moss Landing couldn't even dream about. But those were the Butchers; they came from old East-coast money and had snatched up a lot of land as the country expanded and opportunities presented themselves.

"Where's that baby?" Mil asked.

"Not so much a baby anymore," Paulie said. Their girl, Willy, would be five years old in December, but she clung to Paulie's leg like a much younger child might.

Mil knelt to greet her and took her hand. "Have you ever seen a swimming pool?"

Willy shook her head and gripped Paulie's leg harder.

"Can I show you mine?" Mil held out her hand and slowly Willy released Paulie and took her grammaw's hand.

As the two walked through the crowd, Paulie yelled, "She doesn't know how to swim!"

"Don't worry!" Mil waved a dismissive hand over her head.

"I can't believe your parents did this," Paulie said.

Beau nodded, taking a sip of some caramel-colored beverage she wasn't sure how he'd already gotten ahold of. "It was Dad's dream. One year when we went back to Philly to visit some family, he saw one inside some country club and he's had it in his head ever since."

"Hi there, son." Bob clapped Beau on the back hard. Beau coughed on his drink, then greeted his father. The two soon got into a conversation about the Reds and Paulie found herself wandering off, looking for a drink of her own and maybe a bite to eat.

After checking on Mil and Willie, Paulie meandered through the crowd toward the buffet tables covered in red and white checkered tablecloths. She nodded and politely said hello to people who greeted her, but really she would have been happier at home in her garden. Yes, she'd been the life of the party, but motherhood, and especially single motherhood when Beau was away at war had left her drained. She hadn't the energy for small talk or inside jokes. Sometimes gossip though.

She filled her plate with slivers of bbq and a piece of apple pie and sat on the edge of the pool. She slipped her shoes off and put her feet in. Willie splashed around the shallow end with some other children and Mil caught her eye and winked. Paulie cut into her pie and savored the bite. Whomever had made it had done right by not allowing it to be overtaken by sugar. She could still taste the apple mixed with cinnamon.

"Good, ain't it?"

Paulie stiffened at the sound of Beau's Uncle Billy's voice. "Mm-hmm," she agreed, her mouth still full. She swallowed. "Hi, William." Only his nephews and Mil, his sister, were allowed to call him Billy.

The man sat next to her. A cloying booziness wafted off him. His eyes were glassy and his movements either too slow, or too precise as he tried to clumsily maintain control of himself. "Beau abandoned you, did he? Thasssa mistake. Big. Huge."

"He's just over there, talking to his dad." Her plate was still mostly full and so was her drink. She hadn't a clear way out of this conversation, so she stuffed more pie in her mouth and kept her eye on Willy. Willy tended to provide ample opportunity for Paulie to excuse herself.

"Whatcha been up to Paulie Duhn?" William insisted on never calling her by her married name as if she hadn't earned her way into this family yet.

"Oh, you know, she keeps me busy most days." She set her plate aside and splashed some water on her calves and forearms.

"Kidsss'll do that." William took another swig of his drink, then set his hand on hers and squeezed. She scooted away, laughing nervously.

"Aw, come on. You're such a pretty girl." He reached for her again.

She stood so quickly her drink topped over, staining the cement a bright red color. "Shit."

"Lookie what you did! Mil's gonna be mad."

"I'll chance it, I think. I need to go get Willy some dinner."

"My namesake, you mean?"

Paulie stopped, midstep. "She's not your namesake, William."

He snorted. "Whatever you say, Ms. Duhn."

"Her name is Wilamena, after my great-grandmother," she argued, not that it mattered. William slumped forward, a contented smile greeting his sunburned cheeks.

Paulie rounded the pool and called Willy out of it.

"Mommy, no! I don't wanna get out now."

"I know, honey. But you need to eat something."

"I said, NO!" Willy screamed, her little fists balled.

Paulie brushed her hair behind her ear, a flush of embarrassment creeping up her chest. "Young lady, get out of that pool right now."

The sound of shattering glass punctuated her sentence.

"Jesus! Fuck, Dad. I'm trying!"

Oh no.

Paulie turned and saw Beau, red-faced and gesturing wildly at his father. She hiked up her skirt and stepped into the shallow end. She knelt in front of her daughter and explained, "Not now, Wilamena." Hoping the girl was old enough to understand what using her full name meant. She seemed to grasp it, and offered no more argument as Paulie took her hand and led her out of the water.

The crowd had stilled, all eyes on her husband as he berated his father in front of some of the most important people in the community. This would not end well, but as she stepped in front of him, between the two men, one calm and one screaming, she felt relieved to not be the only one seeing how much Beau Butcher had changed.

Paulie watched her little girl run from ash tree to ash tree in the area around their cottage, playing some game with the fairies the girl swore were out there. She turned from the back door and sat at the kitchen table, her chair grating against the wooden planks of the floor.

Bills cluttered the surface top, stacks of them. They never stopped coming and Beau, well, after he came back from the war, he had trouble keeping a job. Had trouble doing much of anything to be honest. The party last night had just been another example. She wondered some days if it would be better if he'd just died back there in Germany, might've been easier for everyone, but she never said it out loud. She may have been a little outspoken, but she understood some words crossed lines she could never come back from, and she was pretty sure wishin' your husband dead was one of 'em.

Paulie knew how to grow things and the past two winters, it had been the only skill keeping them alive. The problem was the damned trees. They surrounded their lot and only one little spot got enough sun to grow vegetables. Paulie tended it like her life depended on it because...it did.

Yet, an even more important plant grew out there— her hibiscus. She'd paid a hefty price for it while Beau was away. He hated the thing. Hated how she had to give it special care, moving it in and out of the shed at certain times of year. Babying it a bit. But its petals helped keep her without child. Well, that and her meticulous calendaring of her fertile days, making sure to sneak an extra two or three fingers of her moonshine into Beau's nightcap on those days as well. If he knew the lengths she'd gone through to never have another baby, well, she wasn't sure what he might do.

Not having another child had become a sore spot between Paulie and Beau. He expected a whole gang of kids filling their cabin by now. Well, he could just keep on wishin'. She'd despised being pregnant, loathed sharing her body in such a way. The trauma of birthing Willy had been enough for one lifetime. Never again did Paulie want to feel like her body could so easily be ripped apart. So she'd gone to the big library downtown, and researched what she'd need to do to stop it from happening again. It was difficult to even find anything written about it. But one of the librarians had helped.

Bang! Above her head, the floorboards creaked. He was awake, fumbling and shuffling around their bedroom from the sounds of it. Paulie organized the bills. He didn't like to see them all laid out like this, always perceiving it as an afront, some passive aggressive commentary on his inability to keep them secure.

"Fuck it," Paulie whispered and re-scattered the papers. If he chose to be offended, so be it. The dance around his mood was exhausting. And she was so tired of handling everything alone anyway.

His steps thumped down the stairs. She could already hear his breathing and that smacking sound he made each morning as he opened and closed his mouth for no apparent reason, like some fish that had been caught and pulled outta water.

She got up from the table to ready him a bowl of oatmeal. She mixed in the plum sauce she'd made from the last of the wrinkled fruit left in their cellar. She poured a cup of Roosevelt coffee for him and left it on the table. He came into the room, scratching his belly and stretching like a cat.

"Mornin'" she said, with no feeling in it. Nothin' too good 'bout it.

"Can't you at least clear the table while I eat?"

"It's not enough that I cooked and plated you up?" she asked.

He met her gaze then. A dangerous glint flashed, one that hadn't been there before the war but now stowed away for moments like this. Paulie had never tested it though. She saw it and always backed down, feeling like this marriage had turned her into someone else.

He swiped the bills from the table, sitting down to his meal while they parachuted to the floor. Paulie clenched her teeth, biting back the scream that built inside her. Quietly, she knelt and picked up the papers. The tension in the room was so thick she felt nearly choked by it.

"What can we pay this month?" she asked, unwilling to let the pressure bend or break her.

His spoon clattered against his bowl. "Jesus, Paulette,"—he never called her Paulie anymore—"I only just woke up."

"Yeah, and it's nearly ten o'clock. We've got a stack of unpaid bills, and our stores are dwindling. I can't keep doing everything for all three of us."

He rose quickly, his chair banged against the floor. Paulie stood, matching his speed but staggered backward, instinctively positioning herself closer to the back door. Suddenly his hands were on her, gripping her biceps, squeezing in a way that felt like a warning.

"That ain't your job, woman." He practically hissed. Spittle flecked his unshaven chin. The cleft she once loved to press her finger to, now as dark and thorny as an overgrown blackberry brush. "You're only s'posed to cook and keep this house picked up and pop out babies. None of which you do very well." He released her with a slight shove, the small of her back smacking into the counter. A few moments passed between them, their eyes locked.

"Then leave," she said, merely a whisper.

He heard her though, the little zap of her words pressing into his comprehension.

"Leave," she said, louder this time.

He stepped back, seemingly confused, as if the thought had never occurred to him—that he didn't have to be here, that she didn't want him here.

"Leave!" she screamed it this time. Her fists balled at her sides, the release of what she'd bottled up for endless months stiffening her resolve.

"Paulie?"

She laughed. Oh, of course, now he'd use her nickname. The one he used to whisper in her ear as they made love next to the pond. Well, those days were over and there was no going back.

"Just go, Beau. When she's old enough, I'll tell her you died in the war or a car accident. This"—she gestured between them—"is already over."

He looked as though he might argue. "But the cabin? It was my granddaddy's."

"How close were you to hitting me just now?" Paulie asked.

That did it; her words broke through whatever walls he'd built up around himself after the war. For a moment, she saw the boy she'd fallen in love with. The one who'd laughed so freely. Beau walked out of the kitchen, and she followed. He grabbed his coat at the door. "I did love you," he said, but he didn't look back, even when she said, "I did love you too."

Five

Cars lined the street and a flagger waved drivers through a gate. Truly pulled into the Grove's "parking lot" which was really just an open field, tires bouncing over the mounds of grass and loose dirt. Her mother nervously bit the cuticles around her thumb as she eyed the traffic with a glint of suspicion, or maybe it was competition. Truly put the car in park, and Elly jumped out before she could get the keys in her purse.

"Jeez, Mom. We made it, calm down."

Elly marched down the aisle of parked cars. Truly had never seen her move so fast, except at every other flea market, or auction, or antique store they'd visited. Truly hoped she had her phone on her so they could connect when Elly was ready to leave, otherwise Elly'd be on her own for a ride. Not like Elly couldn't find someone to help her though. She'd lived here her whole life, never left the county for more than a few nights.

Vendor's pop-tents dotted the horizon with bright whites and royal blues. Elly disappeared among the crowd, swallowed up like that very worm the early bird always got. Truly smiled to herself, picturing her mother's face on a scrawny, wriggling worm.

"And what are you smirking about?" an elderly-sounding voice asked.

Truly turned to see who'd spoken. Susan Parrish hobbled behind her, using a cane as an aid. She'd nearly become unrecognizable, given how thin she'd gotten, her cheeks gaunt and sunken. But the ring on her finger, a big emerald bauble that Truly had always secretly wanted to try on, gave her away.

"Susan!" Truly exclaimed. She almost asked how the woman was doing but refrained given her appearance and Elly's proclamation of pancreatic cancer last night. Instead, she said, "It's good to see you!" And meant it.

"What's dragged you back to this hellhole?"

Truly laughed. Susan's spunk had always reminded her of Grammaw Willy. "Oh, you know, the usual. Shitty end to an even shittier relationship."

"And now you're staying with your mother."

Truly nodded and held out her elbow for Susan to gain further purchase among the uneven lawn filled with hidden bumps and divots. Susan took it, her arthritic grasp stronger than Truly expected.

"Be careful with that one," Susan warned. "She could wear nails down to nubs with her constant nitpicking."

"I'm aware." Truly laughed. "I need to save money though. I gave a lot up to be with Phil."

"So you're looking for work?"

"Know of any?"

"Well, yes. So happens I've got this terminal disease and am having trouble making it out to the greenhouse each morning. Would you be interested in helping a dying woman out?"

"When you put it that way, how could I say no?"

"Good. It's settled then. I need someone out there watering and running the register and what not from seven to three, Thursdays to Sundays. That work for you?"

"S-Sure." Truly stumbled over the fact that a job had literally dropped out of the ether, but that's the way things happened in small towns sometimes. You knew somebody your whole life, and they helped you when they could, even when they were facing death.

"Alrighty then. Drop me off here at the picnic tables. I need a minute."

A line of sweat had broken out across Susan's forehead. Little beads of perspiration crowned her heavily powdered face. Truly slowed her pace and maneuvered toward the pavilion.

"You want a lemonade? Or an iced tea?" Truly asked as Susan slowly lowered herself onto the bench seat.

"No, no. You go on and find yourself a good deal on somethin' pretty. I'll see ya on Thursday mornin'."

"Okay, if you're sure?"

"Yes, darlin'. It was good to see you, now get!"

Truly walked among the tents, scanning the tables filled with miscellaneous treasures and junk. These types of events were a bit overwhelming for her. While she saw the appeal of sifting through piles to find that one thing that might be mislabeled, or maybe stumbling upon the singular seller who wasn't aware they had something valuable, the idea of haggling a price repelled her. She stepped out of the way of a man carrying a large box filled with trinkets. He bumped into her anyway.

"Watch it!" he yelled as glass items in his box clanked together.

"Back at ya, buddy," Truly mumbled.

She thought of grabbing a coffee, but the line was terribly long, so she kept walking. The dirt path meandered throughout the grounds toward the old baseball fields. There, people had scattered themselves among the wooden bleachers, already sifting through and showing off their finds, while sharing pink boxes of donuts from one of the food trucks near the dugout. Truly's stomach rumbled; a donut might be something she'd be willing to wait in line for. She made her way to the fuchsia truck and got in line.

The woman in front of her reeked of jasmine perfume. Truly brought her fist under her nose, trying not to cough when a flicker of movement beyond the outfield caught her eye. Someone stood out there, hunched over. They looked back and Truly's breath caught in the back of her throat. Her mother snuck along the fence line, creeping around as if she was hiding. *What the hell?*

Truly stepped out of line and cut around the field, keeping a close eye on her mother. Elly crouched low and swooped her head from side to side. After a quick pause, she scampered toward a nearby tree and disappeared behind it, like a frightened animal.

Elly flitted to another tree, closer to the woods encircling the Grove, and hid behind it. Truly picked up her pace, jogging past the dugout. Her purse banged against her hip, keys jangling inside. She needed to get to her mother before she disappeared into those woods. Any manner of things could happen in there, the foremost being that Elly would be more difficult to find. But also, what if she tripped and fell and broke a hip? Phrases like *24-hour assistance* echoed through Truly's mind.

"Mom!" she called.

The sky was gray, and a mist had started accumulating on Truly's skin and clothes. She pushed damp strands of loose hair off her cheeks. Truly passed the outfield fence. She'd lost sight of Elly. Of course this would happen. Of course her mother would lose it and make her chase her around the Grove. Of course she'd get stuck in this town taking care of her. She called for Elly again, edging closer to the tree line.

The forest was dim already, unwelcoming. She scanned the area, hoping for some clue to the direction her mother had gone, when a sparkle of teal light flickered just ahead of her. Instinctively she took a step toward it, then paused, remembering the lights from the night before. What was happening here? Her mind whirled around the fantasy of fairies, who were usually not all that helpful.

"Mom, this isn't funny! Come out of the woods!" She waited, hoping for a response but got none. Elly couldn't have just disappeared, and Truly would have seen if she'd turned back toward the Grove. No, she was in there...with the twinkling blue-green lights that just kept appearing.

Truly rummaged through her purse and pulled out her phone. She flipped on the flashlight and then had a better idea. If she called her mom, she might be able to hear her phone ringing in the quiet woods. Truly stepped under the trees and their stillness covered her shoulders like a shawl. She shone her light over the ground, checking for footprints or some clue as to her mother's directionality, but the grass seemed undisturbed. Truly searched her contacts for "Mom" and pressed the call button.

In the distance she could make out the telltale obnoxiousness of her mother's chosen ringtone. The discordant *bing-bang-bong* made its way to her ears, and she set off in that direction, picking her way through the brambles and moss. Her mother didn't answer, which was disconcerting. When her voicemail picked up, Truly ended the call and tried again. Again, the ringtone could easily be heard among the stillness of the woods. Her leggings snagged on a tangle of thorny dead branches, the fabric tearing. As she worked to untangle herself, thorns pricked the pad of her thumb.

"Damn it, Mom," Truly muttered. A bead of blood formed, and she stuck her thumb in her mouth, the little iron tang singing over her tongue.

The phone stopped ringing, and she tried calling again. But this time it didn't work. She must have lost service moving deeper through the trees, so she made an educated guess about direction and kept looking for clues. Finally, she spied one of the earrings her mother had been wearing near the base of a tree trunk. She picked it up, the brassy metal wet in her palm. The mist had changed into a full-blown sprinkle now, as rain collected in the leaves above her making a soft *put-put-put* sound.

"Mom!"

Truly tried her phone again—nothing. She looked around and a spot of white caught her eye a ways off. She hurried over, and couldn't help but think, this was it: she was about to find her mom in a mangled heap, broken ankle, or worse, from a slip. She could practically feel cuffs tightening around her ankles and wrists. She'd always known her mom felt more like a prison than home.

As she ran toward the flash of color, Truly caught glimpses of red mixed in. And the white itself, wasn't the flat, matte cotton of her mother's shirt, but the furry pelt of some animal. She stopped a mere two feet from the ruined carcass of what was once a rabbit, flung on the ground like some grisly puppet. The poor thing's belly had been torn open; its insides removed.

Truly breathed through her mouth, not wanting the gore to assault her nose. It had to be some bird of prey; the neatness of the disembowelment suggested as much. The white fur was tinged with blood, specks of it dusting the fur around the animal's face and ears. Truly tried to avoid looking at it. Just the idea of its dead eyes sent the coffee she'd drank this morning gurgling back up her throat.

She startled at a rustling sound behind her and looked around. *Fuck, what if it hadn't been a bird?* That meant both she and her mother were out here in the woods with some other predator. She needed to get out of here, but she couldn't leave her mother behind.

"Truly?" a feeble voice called out. "Honey, are you here?"

"Oh thank god. Mom, where are you?"

"Over here."

The shakiness of her mother's voice registered. Something was wrong. Truly pressed forward through the brambles to find her mother, sitting, back propped against a tree trunk.

"Mom!" Truly ran to her mother, touched her shoulder and that's when she saw the blood, a deep maroon, near black, soaking through her mother's shirt. "Oh Jesus!" Truly crouched next to Elly, trying not to imagine how some wild animal had just gutted her own mother. How she'd been too late to save her.

But as Truly examined Elly she found no injuries. The sliming, stinking intestines Elly gripped in her hand and held dearly against her chest where not her own. Truly looked up, her mother's eyes were wide with some wonder Truly could not fathom. Blood speckled her cheeks and lips. She smiled as if she were looking beyond Truly, at some great mystery solved.

"He told me it would be here. I thought I lost it," Elly said. And before Truly could stop her, Elly twisted the rabbit's intestine around her throat as if it were a treasure. "Do you like my necklace?"

Six

Truly tripped over her own feet as she scrambled backward away from her mother. Twigs and brambles tore at her leggings and bit at her skin. "Mom! What are you doing? Get that off!"

"I can't now; it's what I've been looking for." The gleam, a twinkle of teal, in Elly's eyes scared Truly. Elly seemed to be in the present, seemed to know who Truly was, wasn't treating her like a stranger at least, but it appeared as though Elly couldn't see and feel the disgusting bit of organ she'd just wrapped around her own neck. Her fingers traced over it as if it were a set of priceless diamonds and not the innards of a recently killed animal. Truly sucked in a deep breath and held it, the pressure building in her chest—a comfort. She had to get her mom out of these woods and without too many people noticing. Elly would not want anyone to know...any of this.

First, she decided on a story. Maybe her mom saw a wounded animal and followed it into the woods, but then maybe it attacked. Yeah, that's it. Now for *the necklace*. She tried another tack.

"Mom, that's not what you think it is. You have to take it off."

Confusion flitted across Elly's features, wrinkling her brow even more. "But o-of course it is. I followed the lights and his instructions."

"Whose instructions?"

"The man in the woods. The one who lives in the lights."

"Mom, there's no man in the woods." But how could Truly really be sure? Elly herself had told her that the neighbor's son had gone missing. Maybe he *was* out here, playing tricks on an old woman for entertainment. But the why, the how—none of that mattered now.

Truly had to focus on getting *the string of intestines* off her mom, and she was scared to just reach out and grab them. What would Elly do in her current state of mind? Truly bet on her mom fighting her, and she wasn't willing to do that— not with the blood from the dead rabbit still drying on her mother's hands. No, she needed to outsmart Elly, in whatever state of mind she currently functioned.

"Mom, I saw the necklace back at the market. The real one, okay? That's not it. What you've got wrapped around your neck isn't the right one." Truly kept her voice even and slowly stood up. "I'm going to go get it for you. But I need you to..." What did she need? She couldn't drag her mother back to the market looking like this. "Wait." Tentatively, she stepped toward Elly, not wanting to scare her off, needing her to trust that she meant no harm. "You wait right here, and I'll bring it back for you," she repeated.

"How will you pick the right one?" Elly searched Truly's

eyes. Her gaze confused and distant, as if she were in some faraway place.

"It's Truly, Mom. Your daughter. You can trust me." She crouched again, to be at eye level with her mother. Kneeling before Elly, Truly went to take her hands, but decided against it, seeing the gore caked under Elly's fingernails. She swallowed, thankful she hadn't eaten anything that morning. "If I pick the wrong one, I'll just try again, okay?" She put her hand on Elly's shoulder instead, careful not to touch the pink twine of rabbit intestine, and squeezed. "I'm going to help you. Can you follow me to the edge of the woods and wait there?" She felt it important to get her mother as far away from the carcass as possible.

Elly nodded.

"Okay then, let's get you up." Elly obliged, using a nearby tree to stand. Truly rifled through her bag and found every old napkin she'd ever collected from a fast-food place and started wiping Elly's hands. The thin paper was useless against the thick and drying blood covering Elly's fingers. She needed water, a whole steaming shower, to get all this off.

"Let's take this off too." Truly indicated the pink and red gore coiled around her mother's neck.

Elly shook her head, adamant.

Should she press it? Truly could just leave Elly here with the intestines wrapped around her neck, but the idea made her queasy. She concluded that whatever spell her mother was under needed to be severed completely before Truly left. Otherwise, what else might she do?

"What do you think that is? Around your neck."

"It's the necklace he told me to find. A strip of velvet with a charm," she practically sang. Her features wrinkled, announcing a look of frustration or annoyance. "He said I gave it away, but all was not lost. What was once lost, will always be found when it belongs to him."

Truly ignored the mention of the man again, deciding to tackle one thing at a time. "You're wrong, Mom. That's not a necklace."

"Oh." Elly looked down at the messy coils splatted against her chest. "But he said—"

"Forget what he said. It was..." Truly faltered, trying desperately to come up with something, anything. "A test! He was testing your abilities to spot the *right* necklace."

"B-but...so then, I failed." Tears flooded her mother's eyes, spilling near her crow's feet.

"It's okay. We don't have to tell him. I'll just go get what you need and bring it back to you. But you have to take the wrong one off now. Leave it here."

At this, Elly delicately unwrapped the severed guts from around her neck, handling them gently, as if, even in her confused state, she knew they had been a precious piece of a living thing. She set them in a bed of pine needles at the base of a tree. Truly considered that they might need to bury it along with the carcass so as not to attract coyotes, but the coyotes would come no matter how deep they dug, and the turkey vultures already circled overhead. They'd take care of the leftovers better than Truly could.

"That's good, Mom. Let's go this way." Truly took her mother's elbow in her hand and guided her back to the edge of the forest. She followed the noise of the market: idling engines and the mingling voices and laughter of the crowd. Soon she spotted the edge of the baseball field, where she'd first seen her mother creeping around, her movements jerky and suspicious. Truly pushed the image from her mind, choosing to focus on getting them out of this mess before trying to process it. She steered her mother away from the field, closer to the lines of tents and tables. She turned to Elly, directing her to the closest tree.

"I'm going to that vendor; see them?" She indicated the closest table, hoping to god she could find a necklace there.

Elly nodded.

"They have what you're looking for," she reminded her mother. Their short trek through the woods seemed to have soothed Elly. Truly felt hopeful, like this would work, communicating with her mother. "I'm going to buy it and bring it back to you. You can watch me the whole time, but it's important you stay here. Don't leave or wander off, okay?"

"Don't leave..." Elly muttered.

Truly bit her lip. This was still a risk. "Even if he tells you to, okay? It's a trick, a test. You have to stay here and let me do this part for you. It's why I'm here, understand? Why I came home."

Elly seemed convinced, content even. Whatever Truly had just said must have pacified Elly's concerns or mistrust. "So what are you going to do?" Truly asked, reconfirming.

Elly repeated her part of the plan. And that would have to do. It was the only way she could think of to get her mother out of this without thrusting her into the lead role of all the town gossip. The woman had spent her whole life here, living within the social bounds of the town, not ever overstepping. Elly's little foray into the woods would absolutely overtake whatever people were saying about Tamara Faye's pedo son. No matter how Truly felt about her mom, she couldn't let that happen, not after a whole life spent within the box. No. Truly would help her mother keep a lid on this.

And if she found out Tamara's son was behind this some-how, she'd kill that fucker with her own bare hands. Maybe she'd wear his intestines like a necklace.

~

TRULY STOPPED AT THE FIRST STALL SHE CAME TO and scanned the table for jewelry.

"That there's silver," the vendor said. He sat behind the table, a piece of old fashioned, striped stick candy hanging out the side of his mouth.

"Mm-kay," Truly muttered. She felt as if she moved in slow motion, like in a nightmare. Her mind whispered *Come on, come on, come on, find something* while her body languished in real time. She quickly checked over the vendor's goods and turned to move on to the next table, hoping that wouldn't set off Elly, when the man spoke again. "You lookin' for somethin' in par-tic-u-lar?"

"A piece of jewelry—a necklace," she blurted. "But I don't see—"

"I got some things I don't keep on the table back here, if'n you wanna take a look. You know quality; I can tell. You've got that look 'bout ya."

He was just reeling her in for a sale, but she didn't care if he had a god damned necklace tucked up his asshole, she'd take it. Well, but then that would only be one degree away from wrapping an intestine around her mother's neck, so maybe not. "I'll take a look at what you've got. But I'm in a hurry."

"Whole world is that, youngin'. Hurry, hurry, hurry. That's all y'all ever do. Scurryin' 'round with those little com-puters an inch away from your face. It's a wonder y'all—"

"Do you have any necklaces or not?" she interrupted, no time for a sermon.

The vendor adjusted the candy stick to the other side of his mouth and crunched. The candy left a teal-green stain on his lips, much like those damned lights she kept seeing, and the air around him smelled of spearmint masking a kind of chemical tang. He pulled a small wooden box out from under his canvas folding chair. It took a fair amount of effort for him to stand, and all the while Truly kept checking the line of trees, praying her mother had stayed put. The man steadied the chest under his arm and cleared a spot on the table before setting it down.

"I found this piece at an estate sale few years back." He coughed, a little bit of a wheeze sounding underneath it, and sniffed. "'Xcuse me, damn misty weather sets my asthma off." He coughed some more and pulled a handkerchief out of his back pocket. "Go 'head." The man was overtaken by a spasm of coughs. His whole body racked and hunched by it.

"Do you have an inhaler or something?" Truly asked, already fingering the chest's metal latch.

He waved her on, pulling an inhaler out of another pocket of his bib overalls. He shook the thing and sprayed, gulping in the medicine and holding his breath a few beats. "Open it," he rasped.

Truly did as he said and pulled back the lid. "Perfect," she murmured. A necklace of velvet ribbon with a cameo charm attached, unceremoniously laid at the bottom of the box. She ran her finger over the cameo's smooth shell, wondering if it was real. Something about it seemed familiar, but she couldn't put her finger on it, nor did she have the time.

"I'll take it," she said, bypassing the usual haggling of the flea.

A glimmer of greed glinted in the man's eye as Truly realized her mistake. He'd overcharge her, but to hell with it. When one's mother waited bloodied and confused in the woods, one paid whatever damn price to get her out of there with some dignity intact.

"What do you want for it?" she asked.

"Well, now...that's a special piece." He ran his thumbs under the straps of his overalls and looked off into the middle distance, as if he didn't already know exactly how much he wanted. A charade.

"Look, it's basically just a piece of ribbon. The cameo might be legit, but probably not. I can literally go to any other table and find something suitable. I'm not picky about what the necklace looks like, I just need a necklace." *To convince my mother that a string of rabbit intestine is not what she's looking for*, she thought and winced. "Name a price."

"Hundred."

She only had about two hundred and fifty in her bank account, but she'd secured a job; money was coming. "Sold."

The man smiled, and the candy stick in his mouth shifted toward the ceiling of the pop tent. Truly pulled out her credit card and the man brought out his reader, and the deal was done in seconds.

"You can have the box too," the man added.

"Throw in that blanket?"

The man pondered for a moment, pursing his lips in thought, then agreed. "Only 'cause you didn't lowball me on that necklace. It really is somethin' special."

"Great, thanks." Truly closed the box and carried it and the rolled up wool blanket back out of the market, past the baseball field, toward the line of trees where she hoped her mother still waited.

As she neared the woods, she called out, "Mom!" She approximated which tree she'd left her behind, but when she checked Elly wasn't there. "Mom! I've got your necklace. Mom, please." The final word came out as a whisper, a prayer. She needed to get Elly home. She needed to think—process what she'd seen today, even though she wasn't sure she'd ever understand. "Mom?" Finally, Truly heard movement, the shush of pine needles under foot. Her mother appeared, looking as ghastly as ever.

Truly set the box on the ground and wrapped the blanket around her mother's shoulders. It smelled of must and yeast.

"There ya go."

Truly pulled a couple twigs out of Elly's hair. Her mother's eyes never stopped moving, searching.

"It's me. Your daughter."

"I know who you are," her mother practically spat. "I'm not stupid. Where's the necklace? You told me I had the wrong one. You lied, didn't you? You want to keep it for yourself. I should've known not to trust you." Elly's voice rasped with the decades of smoke she'd sucked down her throat.

"I've got it here." Truly turned and picked up the box from the ground. She opened the lid and showed her mother what she'd just bought. "I found it for you."

Elly's eyes shined with wonder as her fingers delicately picked the ribbon out of the case. "It's the one. Oh, I remember it now. Help me put it on?" she asked.

"Of course." Truly set the box down again and took the necklace in hand. She hadn't really inspected it at the vendor's booth. The maroon velvet was old and worn pink in some places. Truly stood behind Elly as she swiped her hair up. Truly stifled a dry heave at the bits of gore still left on her mother, the smell of fecal matter and rotting meat almost too much to bear. She held her breath and affixed the necklace's latch.

"There. Now let's get you home."

Elly pulled the blanket close around her shoulders and agreed. Truly sent a quick prayer of thanks to the gods when her mother didn't fight her over leaving. She seemed to understand the day was done, the market a wash. Yet maybe Elly had received exactly what she came for.

Seven

Elly didn't say a word the whole way home and neither did Truly. What was there to say? What she'd witnessed had been horrifying and scary and had consequences that reached far into whatever future Truly might have imagined for herself. As she swerved over and through the back roads to their ancestral home, she tried to convince herself it was an honor to be able to take care of her ailing mother for an unfathomable number of years. Not a burden. She could push down how her mother made her feel about herself for this time in her life; it was the Midwestern way, for fuck's sake.

As Truly parked in front of the house, Elly stirred. She touched the piece of fabric around her neck and whispered, "Thank you."

"You're welcome. Now, let's run you a bath." Truly stepped out of the car and muttered, "And burn your clothes."

Truly helped Elly out of the passenger seat and up the rickety porch steps. She unlocked the front door and led her mother directly to the bathroom, where she turned on the water and squeezed some bubbles her mom had sitting on the edge of the tub into the stream. The room filled with the scent of lilac, which was much better than the scent Elly had lingering about her—that sickly sweet tang of blood and meat gone bad.

"Okay, Mom. Do you need me to help you get undressed?"

Elly examined herself in the mirror above the sink. She pressed her hair back from her forehead, extended her neck, then smoothed the loose folds of skin. *Could she see the gore left behind*? It didn't seem like it.

Elly frowned. "Why would I need your help?"

"Just asking. It's been kind of a weird morning." Truly tested Elly's memory, but no recognition crossed her mother's features. She seemed blind to it all. "Let me at least take the necklace—"

"No!" Elly recoiled, slamming her hip into the side of the sink. "Ouch, fuck! Look what you made me do!"

"Mom, I didn't—"

"Get out! Get out of here! Stop hovering! I can take a bath by my fucking self!"

"Fine." Truly stepped backward into the hall. Her mother slammed the door. "Fine!" Truly slapped the wall beside the door, anger rumbling up and out of her. "Leave your *bloodstained* clothes out here, *Mom*, and I'll take care of them for you." Sarcasm and resentment dripped throughout her tone, but she'd had it. She'd just saved her mother from being the town gossip and this was her repayment.

Well, great. *Welcome to your new life, Trulia Jane. Look what you've won! An ungrateful bitch of a mother!* Just great.

Truly went downstairs and set about making more coffee.

It was going to be a long-ass day. What the hell was she supposed to do next? Call her mom's doctor? Would they even give her information? She'd probably need to make an appointment and take Elly. Luckily, her mother still kept that kind of shit written in a book instead of in her phone, which was password protected. Truly went to the side table in the living room and opened the drawer. Her mom's little book of phone numbers sat right on top of a stack of what looked like unpaid bills.

The pipes groaned somewhere in the ceiling. She heard a door open and guessed Elly's clothes would be waiting for her at the top of the stairs. Good.

Truly scanned her mom's contacts until she found a number for a Dr. Appleseed and snapped a picture of the phone number. At the bottom of the page, her mother had scribbled a doodle of a rose. Elly had always kept different mediums of art as a hobby. The house was full of her crafts—yarn weavings, pastoral watercolors, lumpy vases she'd thrown in some pottery class put on by the community center.

Truly thumbed through several pages, looking for more drawings. The rose's stem continued along the bottom edge. Truly kept turning pages and a kind of animation presented itself. The stem grew thick at the base; thorns, needle sharp, threatened to come off the page and prick Truly's finger. An underground view of the rose's tangled root system came next. The roots twisted and twined around each other until she realized they formed letters: H-E C-O-M-E-S F-O-R M-E.

Truly's breath hitched in her throat. She slammed the book shut and tossed it back into the drawer. How long ago had Elly drawn that? She guessed "He" was the damn man

Elly had blathered on about at the flea market. How long had her mother's grip on reality been slipping? Truly gave herself a moment. She pressed her fingers to her temples, a paltry attempt at lowering her anxiety around what might be happening to her mother. She lowered her shoulders, which she was sure had been up around her earlobes for hours now, then went back upstairs for Elly's clothes; she really was going to burn them.

Outside the door, she knocked lightly. "Mom, you okay?"

"God damn it, yes! Now leave me alone!"

Truly sucked in a deep breath and held it a few seconds, letting the pressure build in her chest before blowing it out through her nose. "I'll be out back, okay?"

"Fine by me!"

Truly gathered the stinking clothes and blanket in her arms and headed out to the woods, off to the firepit near the shed. They used it for whatever needed to be burned: leaves, yard waste, old broken furniture...ruined, bloody clothing, apparently. She stopped at the falling-down shed and grabbed a bottle of lighter fluid and matches. A burst of gasoline-tinged smell hit the air as she sprayed the clothes. She tossed a lit match on the pile and flames went up with a *whoosh*.

She settled herself on a nearby log to watch. "What a fuckin' day," she mumbled. She called the doctor and attempted to make an appointment, but only got voicemail, being that it was the weekend. She left a message and hoped to get a call back on Monday.

Mindlessly, she clicked on the Pic-A-Sec app and scrolled through her feed, finding mostly ads, until she came upon a post from Phil. There he stood in front of their apartment, looking more than decent in some expensive outerwear. His arms were raised, and he had that little selfie smirk people always did instead of smiling. The caption read "Free at last! Free at last! Thank god almighty I'm free at last." Jesus, what a fucking asshole, rippin' off Martin Luther King Jr. for a break-up post she'd be sure to see. She almost clicked Unfollow but then hearted the picture instead. *Let him wonder what* that *means.*

After a few more swipes, she put her phone in her back pocket. It was only lunchtime. She wished for it to be night —for this day to be over already. As she watched the flames lick over her mother's near-charred clothing, she went back over everything her mother had said while they were out in the woods, trying to get a handle on what she was dealing with here. *The man in the woods. The one who lives in the lights.* At the time, Truly hadn't much time to consider it, her mind immediately jumping to the neighbor's fugitive son. But that last sentence—*the one who lives in the lights*—that was...odd. What on earth could she have meant by that? Yet Truly'd seen lights in the woods too. Those glowing teal specks that had mimicked the lightning bugs, had surrounded her just last night. And she'd seen it again this morning, and again for just a moment when she had been trailing her mother. Was that...something?

"You're gonna burn the forest down if you don't put that out soon."

Truly, lost in her thoughts, jumped. "What—Jesus, Mom. You didn't have to sneak up on me like that."

"Who's sneaking? I called your name twice. At some point, you'll wanna go through the shed. I saved some of my mom's stuff for you."

"You did?"

"Don't sound so surprised. I'm not a total sociopath."

Elly's wet hair was slicked back from her forehead, and somehow her face appeared smoother. The heavy lines and wrinkles Truly had surveyed the night before? Gone. Likely the result of some expensive skincare regimen Elly couldn't really afford and was paying QVC monthly for. Truly's gaze inadvertently dropped to where the image of pink, slimy guts had snaked their way around Elly's neck, and there was the velvet choker, its little cameo dangling.

"You're wearing it," Truly observed, not really meaning to say anything out loud.

"Of course I am." Elly touched her fingers to the charm. "I'm never taking it off."

"Did you clean it though? It was pretty nasty." Truly wavered about whether to mention what and why it was so filthy, finally deciding against it. "Might have bedbugs."

"It does not!" Elly looked aghast.

"You never know with those sneaky little buggers." Truly smiled, trying to communicate that she was teasing.

"Ugh, fine. Now you've got me all paranoid." Elly's fingers went to the back of her neck and unclasped the necklace. "Put that fire out."

"Will do." Truly stood and went to the shed. She grabbed a bucket and took it to the spigot. Water sprayed and splashed into the pail. Elly turned to head back to the house, but in that tiny glimpse of an in-between moment, Truly could've sworn the shadows under her mother's eyes grew as dark as night and her forehead weighed heavy with lines.

Eight

MOSS LANDING, 1949

Paulie was struggling. It had been more difficult than she'd imagined, being on her own. Beau had been gone for many months, and they'd gotten through the worst parts of winter but without the help of one of her neighbors and the Baptist church down the way, Paulie wasn't sure she and Willy would have survived.

After Beau left, her own father denied her. Said it was her place to keep a man, and if she couldn't even do that, she was good for nothin'. Her mama slipped baskets with fresh bread and fruit on the doorstep though. At least Paulie figured it was her mama, finding some small way to defy Daddy.

They'd lost power for a bit last month. Had been makin' do with candles and fires in the hearth. They camped out on the sofa, Willy curled up next to Paulie, sharin' each other's warmth. Paulie wasn't sleepin' no more anyway. Or the little sleep she did get came in fits and starts, either the cramped conditions, the cold, or her worry keeping her awake all hours. Then the pastor had come buy with bags of groceries and some cash to turn the electric back on. He'd offered her work at the church, cleaning up after services three times a week. It brought money in to keep the power on, for now.

"Willy, go put a dress on over your warm clothes, ya hear?" Paulie called from the kitchen.

"Why?" Willy whined.

"Your granny's comin' today." She didn't add how she could be comin' to yank the one thing they did have, the house, out from under them. She didn't add how they could be homeless in a couple of hours. She didn't add that if that happened, she had no idea what to do or where to go.

"Granny who?" Willy asked, standing in the kitchen doorway. The hardships of the last few months had aged her a bit—hollowed out those fat cherub cheeks.

"Granny Mildred, doll. Your daddy's mama."

"How come she never come here before?"

Paulie stopped kneading the dough and took a breath before answering. "Honey, it's hard when someone dies. Especially your baby." She hated lying to Willy about what happened to Beau, but it was easier. To her daughter, Beau died in an accident soon after the war and there'd been no money for a funeral, which was true in its own way.

Willy stood in the doorway now. "Daddy wasn't no baby."

"To us mamas, they're always babies. Now go put something pretty on."

"Okay."

Paulie set the dough aside to rise one more time and chopped everything she had left in storage into a soup for this meeting with her (ex) mother-in-law.

She stirred the vegetables into the broth and looked around, picking up scraps and saving what could be used later. At least the place was clean and orderly. She felt

Mildred would appreciate how she'd taken care of the little home in the woods.

Before she knew it, the house filled with the smell of onions and cabbage and fresh bread. She had only a moment to smooth her hair in the bathroom mirror and smudge a tiny bit of lipstick onto her lips and cheeks. Everything was as presentable as it could be, save for the fact that Paulie had chased this woman's son off to god knew where.

Knock-knock-knock.

Too late to ponder anything more, Granny Mildred was here.

Paulie burped up her nerves on her way to let her mother-in-law in; she needed this house. Besides her daughter, it was all she had in the world.

It was difficult to parse the Mil from the last Fourth of July party from the woman who stood in front of Paulie now. Mildred cut an intimidating silhouette in the gloam of the evening light. Her shoulders were straight, and she held them back and high with a strong core that came from years of etiquette training.

"Hi, Mildred. So happy to see you," Paulie said, as she opened her home to the woman who owned it.

"Paulette." Mildred nodded and walked in, surveying the space. The two women stood in the small living area. An awkward silence spanned between them until Willy started hopping down the stairs, one at a time, her feet stomping and clapping against the wood.

"That would be my grandchild, I presume," Mildred said.

Paulie couldn't help but smile. "It is. She's a bull in a china shop, that one."

"Don't smother that quality in her."

"Why would I—"

"In all my years alive, girls don't often get to be loud and clumsy. More should be. Might help change things."

Paulie tilted her head, looking at her mother-in-law in an unexpected light. "Yes, well, I'm not one to be so dainty and mild neither."

"That's why I approved of you for my Beau." A sadness overtook Mildred's features at the mention of his name.

"Oh, I—"

Willy emerged at the entrance of the stairwell. Her hair had come loose from the braids Paulie had meticulously done up that morning.

"Is this dress okay, Mama?"

She'd selected a too-tight plaid dress with a Peter Pan collar that Paulie had chosen from the donation pile at the church. The orange and yellow pattern highlighted Willy's bright blue eyes and the dusting of freckles across her nose. Her brown hair was the color of buckeyes dropped to the ground in fall. And when she smiled at her grandmother, she had the look of a jack-o-lantern with her two front teeth missing.

"You look perfect," Paulie said.

"Your mama's right," Mildred chimed in and stepped around Paulie. "It's been a while since we've seen each other, but I'm your granny, doll."

"I know who you are. Your daddy's mama."

"That's right."

"He's dead."

At that, Mildred's gaze snapped back toward Paulie.

"The accident after the war," Paulie offered by way of explanation.

Mildred rolled her lips, her chest rising as she took a deep breath. Eventually, she nodded. "Yes, the war took much from us."

Paulie was glad for Mildred's acquiescence in the matter. "Show your granny the book we've been reading, Willy, and I'll get us some tea." Paulie said, moving the conversation away from Beau.

"That sounds lovely," Mildred said. She let Willy take her hand and guide her to the couch. Paulie hoped Mildred couldn't feel the impressions their bodies had made on the cushions.

She excused herself to the kitchen and poured two cups of the tea she'd been saving for this evening. When she cleaned the church, she'd taken to pilfering two sugar cubes each time. She checked them now, to make sure no pocket lint stuck to them, and popped them in the hot tea. She stirred as the sugar melted, letting the repetitive action calm her nerves and listening to Willy read the worn copy of *The Poky Little Puppy* she'd found left behind in the women's restroom at the church.

Willy was a wonder, reading already. Paulie remembered puzzling over letters, trying to force them to be still on the page, but for Willy it seemed like she was born knowing. Words lifted off the page and out her baby's mouth before the girl had turned four.

Paulie tapped the teaspoon on the edge of the cup and lifted the saucers from the table. She entered the living room and set Mildred's tea on the little side table they hadn't torn apart for firewood yet. Granny and granddaughter nestled cozily together on the couch.

Willy closed the book when she was finished, and Paulie told her to go color in her room for a while. The grownups had some talking to do.

"I'm a grownup," Willy said.

"You most certainly are not," said Paulie. "Go color a picture for your Granny to take home with her."

Willy stuck out her lower lip. "Fine."

The two women listened to her clomping footsteps as she ascended the stairs, waiting to speak until she was out of earshot.

"Your girl's about ready for school, I'd say."

"Turned five last December but not soon enough for the schoolhouse."

"She's readin' better than most eight-year-olds. She'll be top of her class, for sure."

Paulie smiled politely. "We'll see."

"We shall." Mildred sipped her tea. "Which brings us to the matter of this property. It's been in my family for a generation. Used to have dirt floors, and I was born right there next to the hearth."

Paulie steeled herself for the blow. A home with so much history would certainly be coveted among the Butcher clan. Beau did have siblings, four sisters and a younger brother.

Mildred eyed the stairwell and spoke low, "I hope you know I don't condone what Beau did here, leaving you alone with the girl."

"I told him to go, ma'am." Paulie winced at her own words. If she wanted to keep the house, she wasn't rightly making a case for herself. But she didn't hold back. "He was suffering here with us. He needed something I didn't have," she whispered so that Willy wouldn't overhear.

"And you told her he died?"

"It's easier that way."

Mildred sniffed and took another sip of her tea. "You pour so much into raising your child. So much time, your whole body. Just to have some tyrant, worlds away, be the cause of ruining them..." She scraped her teeth across her lip, bit down in restraint, staring into the middle distance.

"So here's what's going to happen." Mildred set her nearly emptied teacup on the side table. She straightened her white gloves in her lap. "A new factory is coming to Moss Landing. Associated with the government. I don't know all the details, but I go to the council meetings and they just approved the land rights. Billy, my brother, has already applied for a management position."

"That's great," Paulie said, unsure what this had to do with her and the house.

"You're to start at the new secretarial school in Fairborn and you'll drop Miss Willy off with me each morning. Once you've received your certificate, a job will be waiting for you at the new facility working for Beau's Uncle Billy. You'll pay some rent to me for this place. And that will be that. What do you think?"

Paulie could hardly breathe, let alone agree to the deal. But agree she did, with tears near to spilling onto her cheeks. This was a true lifeline. Not a temporary thing. An opportunity to not only survive, but thrive.

Nine

Several days had passed without incident. In fact, Elly seemed better. Certainly, she seemed happier than when Truly had first arrived. Her negative commentary and nitpicking had nearly stopped. Truly had counted twenty-four whole hours since her weight had been mentioned. Elly looked better too. Her skin didn't seem as pale or dry as it had when Truly first arrived.

From her seat at the dining table Truly watched her mother closely, looking for signs that she should call Susan and cancel coming to work at the greenhouse this morning. But her mother zipped around the kitchen with vigor, pouring coffee for them both, stirring oatmeal until the whole room smelled of brown sugar.

"I'm heading to the greenhouse to help out Susan today, remember?"

"Why do you think I made you a healthy breakfast?"

"So you'll be okay without me here?"

Her mother stopped mid-bite, her spoon hovering over her bowl. "Why wouldn't I be okay?"

That was the thing though. Either Elly didn't remember what she'd done in the forest, or she was purposefully avoiding the topic as if she hadn't ripped a helpless bunny to shreds with her bare hands. As if she hadn't killed that animal merely to drape its innards around her neck.

"Hmmph," she huffed. "I've been out here in these woods my whole life. Don't get all weirdly protective over me after being here a handful of days. I'm not *too old* to function."

Truly would have to lay it out for her mother eventually. The behavior or episode needed to be addressed. But maybe not right before she left for work. She didn't want to send Elly into a tailspin of forced confrontation and then just abandon her. No, she'd wait till this afternoon. She wanted to talk to Susan anyway and see if she'd noticed anything strange about her mother's behaviors recently.

"All right, Mom. Just...keep your phone on you."

Elly waved her hand, shooing Truly's concerns away, then she gripped the cameo pinned to the velvet ribbon at her throat.

Truly noticed how her mother's face had changed. Years of worry and wrinkles and smoking had smoothed seemingly overnight. As her mother's hand played with the charm, she saw how they had transformed as well. The blue ropey veins floating at the surface were gone, the tan age spots dissolved. The back of her mother's hand was as supple and plump as Truly's own.

How can that be?

"What are you using?" Truly asked.

Elly seemed taken aback. "What do you mean? Nothing."

"Your skin...looks so good." Truly moved to grab her mother's hand, but Elly dodged her grasp.

"Just good genetics, I guess."

"Smoother than mine, though?"

"Must've skipped a generation." Elly stuck a cigarette between her smirking lips.

"If you don't want to tell me, fine. I don't have time for your bull shit." She'd told Susan she'd be there early. She scooped the last bit of oatmeal into her mouth and took her bowl to the sink. "I've got to go."

"I'm glad you're helping Susan."

"Me too. Text me if you need anything."

"I won't." Her mother frowned.

"I mean if you need me to bring home anything from the store. I'm gonna drive right by it."

"Oh, well, yes. We may need a few things."

Truly turned back toward her mother and startled. For a brief second, it was as if she looked back in time or at an early portrait of her mother. She blinked and the current setting fell back around her, but...Elly's face. She looked downright lovely.

"What? Why are you staring at me like that?"

"Nothing." But it wasn't nothing. "Like I said, just text me a list and I'll stop at the store." There. At least, she'd come up with a way to touch base with Elly throughout the hours she'd be gone. It wasn't perfect but it was something. And it gave her mother a way to feel like Truly wasn't checking up on her.

Truly walked out of the house and into the surrounding gray-green light of dawn cresting in the woods. She worried about "the man" and the lights he supposedly lived in, what all that really meant, but she had to work. Being with and leaving Phil had drained her savings, and if she needed to be some kind of caretaker for Elly now, well, then money—one must have it.

She looked back one more time and through the window caught the TV coming on. Her mom settled on that plastic surgery show she liked. Okay, good. Zoning out to comfort shows was normal.

Truly stepped off the porch and got into her car, as she backed out of the driveway the light of the TV flickered and faded to a blue-green color in the front window.

SUSAN'S PLACE WAS DOWN THE ROAD, NOT TAKING more than a few minutes to drive there. Her mom had started the greenhouse in her twenties, and a picture of a young hippie with flowing hair and bare feet walking the grounds with a little Susan in pigtails hung over the register station. She'd cultivated a lovely spot over the years, planting a huge swath of wild lupines all around the structure. In the spring it was a sight to behold, the landscape covered in conical blooms of purple and blue. From a bird's eye view, it probably looked like a bruise.

A line of trees edged the backend of the property, but the tops of some of the buildings and the water towers from the old nuclear plant could still be seen over the treetops. Just a gentle reminder that the area was most certainly half-poisoned, no matter the beauty upfront.

Truly parked in the gravel lot and her footsteps crunched all the way to the glass greenhouse. The structure itself looked straight out of a storybook, with a real *Secret Garden* vibe. Through the panels Truly could see the dark emerald green of plant life, but also the studs and frame of the building. She opened the door, and a strip of sleigh bells jangled.

"Hello! Susan?" The greenhouse was already sweltering, and Truly felt as if she might need her inhaler to catch a deep breath. She kept on though, following the pea gravel path as it meandered through the huge glass house, intermittingly calling for her new boss. She grew nervous when no one answered. Susan had looked only slightly healthier than a skeleton at the flea market.

She took a few more steps and gasped when she stumbled upon a body lain on the ground in front of a row of potted marigolds. The upper half of the body sprawled under the bench of plants, so that Truly couldn't quite make out who it was or what was wrong with them.

"Jesus Christ! Susan! Is that you?" Truly ran to the poor woman's side and crouched. She grabbed for, what had to be, Susan's hand and checked for a pulse. She scrambled backward when the hand reacted, and a shout rang out from under the bench. The body wiggled itself backward and Susan, headphones clamped over her ears, emerged from under the marigolds.

"What the hell?" Susan asked, yanking the headphones off.

"I've been calling for you!" Truly managed. "And-and when I saw you lying there—"

"You thought I was dead." Susan shook her head. "Hazard of a cancer diagnosis, I guess. Well, I'm still kickin'! Help me up." Susan held out her hands and Truly stood, then helped Susan get up as well.

"What were you doing under there?" Truly asked.

"Oh! Thought I saw something. Critter. Maybe a rabbit."

Truly stepped back and sucked in a breath, thinking of the one her mother had torn apart over the weekend.

"It's a constant battle with them. They get in and eat my garden plants sometimes before I can sell 'em."

"Oh, what do you do?"

"Well, that's what the marigolds are supposed to be for. Not much to do, 'cept get a dog to just keep trying to chase 'em off. Fluff doesn't do much o' that anymore though." Susan indicated a big heap of tan, curly fur curled up in a dog bed near the register.

"Fluff's still alive?" Truly asked enthusiastically.

"Yup, just like me though, darlin'. One paw out the door already."

"I'm sorry."

"Not your fault. Comes with the territory."

"What do you mean?" Although Truly already knew— the nuclear waste leak, a cover up, and then came all the cancer with no "definitive causal link".

"Oh you know the old stories, don't ya?" Susan leaned heavily on a cane to maneuver around the greenhouse. But the paths were gravel, and it couldn't have been easy. Truly followed her back to the register.

"I know a majority of the graves up at Moss Christian are filled up by cancer, if that's what you mean."

"Grab that hose, hun. Oh yeah, but I mean stories even older than that. Elly never told you? Gosh, when we grew up they were like our very own ghost stories. Elly really never told you? She loved them most of all."

Truly shook her head and hefted the ring of hose over her shoulder. "What needs watering?"

Susan pointed toward a row of green shrubs and unwrapped a butterscotch candy, the gold wrapper crinkling under her fingers. She popped it in her mouth. "*The Girl with No Face, The Dog Gone Bad*? She never told you 'bout them?"

"If she did, I don't remember."

"Oh, you'd remember." Susan adjusted the candy to the other side of her mouth, tucking it into her cheek like a squirrel getting ready for winter. She sat on a cushy desk chair she kept behind the counter, and Truly tried not to notice how she grimaced in pain. "Especially the one...what was it called? Something 'bout those damn twinkle lights people claim to see."

"Twinkle lights?" Truly perked up. She'd seen twinkling lights. Out in the woods. A couple times now.

"Yes, yes." Susan leaned back in her chair, her eyes closed, face tilted toward the ceiling. "What was it called? *The Man who Lived in the Lights*! That's it." Her shoulders shuddered. "Oh, that one was a good one! Somebody even turned that one into one of those little songs we used to chant when we jumped rope back in the day."

Truly, too stunned to respond, turned on the water, aiming for the row of plants in front of her. A light mist emerged from the nozzle and after a few seconds the whole area was wet with it, even the air. She swore she could feel the spray settling at the back of her throat when she breathed. *The man who lived in the lights...* That's what her mother had said. That's who her mother had blamed for what she'd done to that damn rabbit.

"Don't overwater 'em, now!" Susan's voice rang out over the *shoosh*ing spray of mist.

Truly bent and turned off the water and wound up the hose. "Can you tell me that last one? Do you remember how it went?" she asked, trying not to seem too interested, trying to keep her voice even.

"Oh, it was based on some old rumor about some boss at the plant. You know the type, handsy as hell with the female employees." Susan paused and sipped from a travel mug. "Well, one day he grabbed the wrong lady, and she pushed back. Only he tripped over something, maybe his own feet, and fell into the reactor or some vat—I don't know. *Poof!* He's just gone, right? And the lady, well, she walked away, doesn't say a word to anyone."

"No shit," Truly replied, and knelt to scratch behind Fluff's ears. The dog licked her fingers and grunted.

"After some time passes though, people start noticing he's missing. He has a family. His car's still in the lot. There's an investigation, but nothing comes of it. It's as if the man just up and disappeared. Only he didn't. Not completely." Susan crunched the butterscotch between her teeth. Little bits of it landed on the counter and she swept them to the floor.

"See *something*, whatever the hell happened to him, whatever the hell he fell into, changed him. The lady, who never told a single soul what she did, started seeing these little lights around her property at night mostly, but sometimes on a really cloudy, gray day, they'd come. And they made her *do* things." At the counter, Susan piled a bucket and dish soap on top of some stained gardening gloves. "We gotta compost the waste and clean the shelves. Lemme show you what needs taken care of first."

"Wait, what kinds of things did he make her do?" Truly slipped the gloves on.

"Oh, you know, all the gross stuff kids come up with." Susan tried to stand but failed. "Over there, row two. Clear out the dead stuff, and then wipe the shelves down with warm soapy water. The soil in the beds at the ends of rows five through eight needs turned over too."

"But how does anyone even know what she saw if she never told anyone? You can't just tell three-fourths of a story and then send me off to work."

"Technically, I'm your boss. So I can."

"Fine. But how did the jump rope chant go?"

Susan snorted. "I can't even remember."

Truly sulked but went to work thinking Susan's story was a sure sign that Elly was experiencing a mental break, early onset dementia and the like. By some misfiring of the brain, her mother had dredged up a childhood ghost story and committed some heinous act because of it.

She wanted to talk about it. But Susan was Elly's oldest and dearest friend. And her mother's medical issues weren't really something Truly felt comfortable sharing. Although before too long everyone would know something was going on.

She raked the dead stuff into neat piles and carried the bucket to the sink in the back corner. Truly twisted both the cold and hot faucet handles, until a steady warm stream ran from the faucet. She squirted the gooey blue dish soap into the bottom of the bucket and set it under the cascading flow. While it filled, she checked her phone, hoping for a message from Elly's doctor. But only a notification from Phil came up: a text message.

Stopping by your mom's with a box of your stuff today

K was all she typed, all he deserved.

She didn't want to see him. He could rot in hell for all he'd put her through. How he'd slowly isolated her and made her feel like it was everything she wanted and deserved. How he'd treated her as if she were an embarrassment, when really, he was the very obvious piece of shit in the relationship. If she'd kept her friends around, they would've told her to leave him way before she'd given up her job. But she'd ghosted them all at his insistence that they weren't good for her. That they made her drink too much and eat too much and cuss too much. Basically, *live* too much. She'd been fun. She'd been young. And now she was right back in Moss Landing with no one to talk to except her mother.

Her mother. She didn't want Phil going there and meeting with Elly without her being there to run interference. Especially given Elly's current state. Yes, she had seemed better at breakfast, but when someone has torn an animal to shreds with their bare hands the standards for being "better" were minute.

When, she added to the text thread.

Parking now

Shit. Truly checked the time; she'd only been at work a few hours. She had no idea what Susan allowed by way of a break, but everything seemed pretty casual. Truly decided to just tell her most of what was happening: Phil was stopping by, and she felt like she needed to be there. "It shouldn't take long," she added.

"Take whatever time you need, dear. I can run the register."

"Thanks, Susan."

"Flip the sign to Open on your way out and I'll see you later this afternoon."

"Okay, you want me to bring you back a sandwich or something."

"A taco will do just fine."

"You got it."

Truly walked out of the greenhouse and the air felt cool against her cheeks. She took off her flannel and tied it around her waist. She left the greenhouse with an uneasiness settling in her stomach, whether it was Susan's story, her mother's break with reality, seeing Phil, or the nuclear plant topping the trees along the horizon, she wasn't sure. Probably all of the above.

Ten

MOSS LANDING, 1951

Paulie stood at the counter and stirred a packet of sugar into the sludge her boss took for coffee. She could hear him in his office, a one-sided conversation on the phone, his over-loud laugh booming through the walls every now and again. People seemed to love William; she despised the man.

Alone in the waiting area of William's office, she checked his door—closed—then brought the Styrofoam cup to her mouth. She gathered saliva on her tongue and pushed it past her lips, letting it dribble into the man's drink. It was stupid, if she got caught, not even Mildred could save her. She needed this job.

Spitting in the man's coffee didn't bring her dignity back, but it momentarily stoked her spite, and that felt just as good most days.

She set the cup back down and scratched at her calf, hating the way the nylons gripped at her legs all day long. The sensation of being pawed at never seemed to leave her, even when she stripped them off in the evening.

Going into his office, his inner sanctum, was always a gamble. She never knew what to expect. Would he yell at her? Call her crude names? Sometimes she preferred being verbally demeaned to his slinking, dry hand he'd slide against her thigh, acting as though nothing were happening, as if his touch were merely an accident of their approximation. It froze her in place, every time it happened. She couldn't speak, couldn't slap his hand away. Couldn't even pray to a god that he'd stop. When he slid his fingers over the space behind her knee, she was solid ice, a glacier of fear.

She picked up his coffee and readied herself. She crossed the room, standing just outside his office door, and knocked softly.

"Come in," he said. "Just a minute, John. My secretary needs me." His laugh sounded again, the snorting one, a little piglet rooting around in the mud. She could imagine what had been implied on the other end of the phone call. She was one of a handful of women that worked at the plant, and she'd heard all their "jokes".

She stepped into the room and stayed on the opposite side of his desk, setting his coffee amid the reports he was detailing. She had no idea what the man did that took up all eight hours of the workday, but he constantly had her filing, and lately shredding, these reports. She wasn't sure exactly what was going on, but she was smart enough to know that not everything around here was on the up and up. The way she figured it, nearly everyone that worked here had the same inclination, but where else were they gonna go for jobs?

He expected her to stay until he dismissed her, so she did. She crossed her arms and lingered before him, waiting for his shooing wave. Sweat beaded on her upper lip and her neck flushed.

"Okay, yes. John, I can make that happen. You know I can."

...

"Uh-huh. Will do. Bye now." William slammed the receiver into its bed, but it didn't mean anything—Paulie didn't even flinch—that was just the way he moved around in the world, except for when he was touching her. Then he was sly, gentle even. A boy again, stealing a cookie out of the jar before dinner, praying his mommy didn't catch him. It made her sick. She swallowed back bile and waited for instructions.

"I'm gonna need to run a quick inspection of some machinery over in plant three. Grab the paperwork and keep detailed notes."

"Yes, sir." She turned and left the room, heading back out to the safety behind her desk. She collected the correct forms from the metal filing cabinet, sliding and banging the drawer open and shut, then clipped them to a clipboard. These excursions out into the rest of the factory, her trailing behind him, straining to hear over the swish and clank and yelling chatter of employees, were commonplace. He liked her to go with him, always showing her off to people he considered underlings. He wanted them to think they were having an affair, made him feel like a bigger man—this young woman so fully compressed under his thumb. Among the other employees, he laid on the "honeys" when he spoke to her and stood so close she could taste his after-shave and the two cans of Budweiser he allowed himself at lunch.

"Ready?" he asked as he came into the antechamber of their shared office. He adjusted his tie and slipped his gray suit coat back over his shoulders. He never went out into the factory without it, wearing it like armor, a signifier he said, always adding, *Shows them who's boss.*

She couldn't bear it today. She neared her breaking point, felt on edge all the time. "Actually, I'm not feeling well. Can you do this without me today?" she asked.

"What is it? That time of the month? Nonsense. Let's go."

She clenched her jaw at the mention of her period. Of course he would go there. She pressed the clipboard against her chest and grabbed a pen, then followed him out the door. What else was she supposed to do? He'd made it clear time and again, that she was replaceable. That he was doing a favor for his sister. Which meant she'd better be grateful, and she better show it.

# Eleven

Phil had pulled his vintage-inspired, yellow Bronco off to the side of the driveway and parked in the grass. Truly hated how cute it was and had refused to admit she liked it when they were together.

Truly parked next to his car and made her way up the front porch. Before she got to the front door, she noticed an unnatural quiet. Her own footsteps nearly echoed along the planks of the deck. Her keys jangled. This wasn't right; there should be tons of regular forest noise. Hell, she could always hear the *rish-rush* of cars flying down nearby route 27. But just then it felt as though she existed in a vacuum, a bell jar. A moment frozen. A moment orchestrated.

A creeping worry wriggled at the back of Truly's throat. She should have texted her mother. Or warned Phil about her mother's erratic behavior. *Shit.*

Truly tried the door, but found it locked. *Shit.* Not a good sign. Elly never locked the door in the daytime. Truly knew so little about what her mother was going through, or how long she'd been suffering paranoid delusions. And know she'd sent Phil in here like a—*don't think it, don't think it—* rabbit to slaughter.

She fumbled a bit with the keys and unlocked the door. "Mom!" The living room was empty. Only the muted TV played that awful show she liked. She must have recorded them and rewatched them. The horrific scene of a nose job flashed before Truly's eyes before she found the remote and turned it off. "Mom!"

Where were they? She checked the kitchen. Signs of an encounter were scattered across the table: two coffee mugs, her mother's pearly pink lipstick stained the lip of one; a tray of apple crumble, pieces cut out of it; the sticky remains gumming up a small plate and fork. All good signs. No tortured animals. No blood. Truly's anxiety ratcheted down a bit. Her mother had obviously greeted Phil and treated him well. Now if she could only find them.

She went out the back door to check the yard. Maybe they were enjoying the weather on the deck. Or maybe Elly had asked Phil to fix those loose boards framing the shed. She could put anyone to work. That was the old her. And again, Truly let herself relax a little more. Her shoulders sagged, coming away from the bottoms of her ears. Her jaw unclenched. But still, she couldn't find them.

The shed matched the house, with its gray cedar shake siding and cottage windows. A little platform deck led up to the barn-like doors. Truly peeked through the windows. The worktables lay cluttered with tools and half-finished projects. Boxes lined the walls. The dust, undisturbed. She didn't bother to go in; it was clear no one had been in there recently. She turned. And that's when she saw the lights again.

What the hell? She followed the general direction of the trailing teal lights away from the shed. Flashes of what she'd seen at the market played: a ruined corpse, guts nearly the same glistening shade as her mother's favorite lipstick, all that blackish dried blood. She inhaled a long breath, holding it a few seconds before releasing it through pursed lips. She nearly prayed for a snapped twig, the startled flap of bird wings, some other clue as to where her mother, and Phil, might be.

Her ears felt as if they might pop, the pressure building and needing release. When she took another step forward, they did.

A vacuum seal released as if a spell had been broken.

Cars rushed over the highway beyond the mourning woods, and a distant neighbor cranked up a leaf-blower—the sputtering *put-put-put* revving to a roar.

Birds chirruped above her, and a slight breeze whooshed through the leaves. The teal lights dissipated.

"What the fuck?" Truly wiggled her finger in her ear, then stepped backward. The bell jar came back down atop her, or atop some perimeter she could not see. The silence enveloped her, suffocating in the reminder of its nothingness. The lights she'd been trailing reappeared, burning a janky, warped perimeter around the property. She moved forward and all the noise came back, the lights gone.

"What the—" She couldn't finish the thought because that's when the screaming started.

SHE RAN TOWARD THE SOUND, HORRIFIED BY THE shrieking alarm.

What's happened? As her legs carried her forward, images of a fallen Elly—shattered hip, or a knee blown out—flashed through her mind. The forest became a blur of grays and browns and greens and yellows, a paint swirl of color, as she ran back toward the house.

"Mom!" she yelled. "Mom, I'm coming!"

The screams stopped as she passed Phil's parked SUV and thumped up the deck stairs. She threw open the front door and ran straight into Phil's chest. He steadied her with one hand, the other tucked into his waistband.

Truly shook her head. "What are you—" She noticed his hand placement, his pants unbuttoned and his shirt untucked. She shoved him, and he stumbled backward into the living room. "What the fuck is going on here?" Truly advanced, hearing her shaking, rage-filled voice reverberate around the living room. She pushed him again and his hand came out of his pants, a red blotch forming on the inner thigh of his khakis. He braced himself against the arm of the couch.

"I-It's not what you think," he stammered.

"What am I thinking, Phil?" She knew she was snarling, ready to tear this man—nothing more than a piece of meat—apart limb from fucking limb.

"She came on to me."

Truly laughed, madly. Something in her brain loosened; her heart shook free from its protective sac. "My very elderly mother..." She recognized the old mnemonic and laughed again. But then she noticed tears in Phil's eyes. He swiped his hair back from his forehead, a nervous habit.

"I-I can't explain it." He spoke softly, almost to himself. "She looked—gah!" He stomped his foot and seemed to notice his surroundings. "I gotta get the fuck out of here."

"Oh, no. You're not going anywhere." Truly pushed him again and he tripped over the coffee table, falling to the rug.

"She looked like you!" he yelled, holding his forearm over his head in a protective stance. "I thought it was you! Until— her face changed, Truly! It *was* you and then...it was all gray and"—his eyes moved around the room, searching for the right word, searching for the truth, or his version of it at least —"dead looking. I'm telling the truth. I would never, *never* get with your mom."

"Except you did, right? You fucked my mom."

"No-no, I didn't! We didn't have—she just went down —" He brought the heel of his palms to his eyes and scrubbed. "When I realized—when I pulled away, she bit me. Took a fucking chunk out of my leg."

Truly reexamined the maroon stain blooming near Phil's crotch.

"Get out." Her rage had stopped spurting like a volcano, instead it just poured out of her, slow in its advance, sad as it hardened into a rocky mass.

"Your stuff is still in my trunk. Do you want me to—"

"Just leave. I don't ever want to see you again."

Phil stood and straightened his button-down shirt, tucking the front hem back into his bloodied pants. He moved toward the door, so close to Truly she could smell his expensive cologne—musky, cloying.

She stepped aside and then added, "Unless my mom decides to press charges." Phil's hasty forward momentum stopped, his hand frozen on the door knob. "I think what-ever happened here today would easily fall under elder abuse." Truly watched the flushing pink rise from under his collar. "What would your precious partners say about that?"

He swallowed, his Adam's apple bobbing, maybe even trembling. When he spoke, it was a low and tremulous sound, showing a bit of fear, a bit of anger, a bit of something Truly couldn't recognize.

"I can't explain how she tricked me into thinking I was with you, but that's what I really, *really* thought. It isn't elder abuse; *she* assaulted *me*."

Truly didn't want to believe him. She wanted to run to the kitchen, grab a knife, and cut this fucker out of her life for good. But she had her mom to think about. She needed to check on her, get her to a hospital maybe.

"If she wants to call the police, I'm gonna."

He nodded and opened the door, then paused. As if to say something, his mouth opened and closed like a fish gulping breath.

"Say it. You might as well," Truly said.

"I wouldn't have consented to that *thing* up there."

Truly scraped her teeth across her upper lip. As much as she didn't want to think of Phil as a victim, knowing the violence her mother had been capable of just days ago, thinking of how her appearance had changed...it added up.

"Something really messed up is going on with your mom, Truly."

"Yeah, *that* I know. But it doesn't exactly let you off the hook. You are your own kind of monster."

He acted as if he might argue with her, but then gave up. Turning away from her, he walked out the door. His footsteps stomped over the porch, and his car door slammed, then the engine growled.

She stepped to the window and watched the yellow Bronco until it disappeared. Maybe she shouldn't have let him go. Maybe she should have called the police immediately. Gotten Elly an ambulance and let doctors and nurses deal with this situation.

Maybe, maybe, maybe, maybe, maybe...

Twelve

MOSS LANDING, 1951

The moment they walked into the empty plant Paulie knew something wasn't right. Their heels clicked along the cement floor and a prickling sensation bloomed in the back of her throat at the sound of each step. She was alone in a maze of machinery with a man that could scarcely keep his hands off her when other people were around. What would he do, what would he try with only the quiet hum of the machines encircling them?

"Paulette, over here. I wanna show you something."

Paulie's chest tightened, and her empty stomach roiled with anxiety. She swallowed saliva, but imagined it to be bile, welcoming the burns that might save her. Disgust him, if she could puke on demand. As she made her way toward him, her soul slinked out of her body.

She stepped beside him, a wave of heat radiating the whole front of her body. Lava, or what looked like it, roiled in a trench before them. Paulie couldn't take her eyes off the red-orange glow churning at her feet. She saw shapes and figures form in the hot sludge.

"It's the salt pit. Check this out." William brought a can of beer out from his jacket pocket. He opened it, the tab cracking the aluminum with a *tck-tsh*, and slurped the foam along the edge. He offered Paulie a drink, but she declined.

"More for me," he said and gulped. In seconds, he'd crushed the can in his fist and tossed it toward the coffin-shaped pit. It disappeared, the slurry burning a golden-orange for a few seconds where the can had just been.

"What'd'ja go and do that for?" A voice called from somewhere behind them. Paulie turned to see a woman in overalls, sweat staining a navy-blue handkerchief that hung around her neck. "You can't go throwin' metal in there. We'll have to drain the pit now." She'd chewed an apple to the core and tossed it into the pit as she joined them.

"You just threw something in there," he huffed. "Why can't I?" He straightened the lapel of his suit and stood a little taller.

"Sure, but apple cores don't leave nothin' behind. Your can will. And it'll fuck up the cast of the ingots if it's not cleaned outta there."

Paulie bit her lip to keep from smiling. She wanted to run over and hug this woman. Instead, she asked, "Should I add that to the notes, sir?"

"You better," the woman said, her tone factual and flat.

"No!" William yelled.

He cleared his throat. "Do not write any of this down."

"How you gonna 'splain the need for overtime then? We just cleaned out that pit, shouldn't need to do it again for some time yet."

William paused. Paulie knew he wasn't used to being reprimanded at work, especially by a woman. A flash of pink crept around his collar and spittle gathered at the corner of his mouth. She tried to warn the woman, make eye contact or some other gesture that would communicate the need to back off.

"Well, I'm the boss so I can *'splain* it however I see fit. Paulette, make a note that this employee,"—he exaggerated bending over to see the name stitched the woman's overcoat — "Dorothy, was seen lingering near salt pit three today and someone saw her throw a can into the slurry. Note that it'll need to be drained and cleaned, like she said, and write her up for the incident."

"But—" Paulie started, and William grabbed her elbow with more force than he ever had.

"Do it," he spoke through gritted teeth.

Paulie tripped over her heels when he let her go, and the yawning maw of the open pit flashed a hot warning. This was not the place to get into a fight with her boss. Her brain screamed, *Danger*! She pretended to scribble what he'd told her, as if she'd ever forget what happened.

"And you," William turned back toward Dorothy. "You're fired!"

"No, I'm not," she said, simple and plain, which infuriated William even more.

"Oh yes, you are!" He grabbed for the woman, but she feigned sideways out of his grip.

"You can't fire me. And you can't lie about me neither," Dorothy said, as cool as if the three of them were having a picnic on a fine spring day and not standing precariously close to a hell pit.

He laughed, ran his palm over his buzz cut. "You can't stop me."

"I have a witness." Dorothy stared right at Paulie, challenging her to accept the position.

Paulie looked away. She had a child to think of; she needed this job.

"Her?" William shrieked with laughter. "Oh you've miscalculated the situation, missy. That girl ain't your witness. She works for me. She'll do whatever I say." His arm slithered around Paulie's waist. He pulled her in front of him. She could feel the disgusting lump of him pressed into her behind. His breath was on her neck, in her ear. She'd dropped the clipboard in the commotion and had nothing to hold onto but her own self. William placed a wet kiss on Paulie's neck, this time bile did burn up the back of her throat. He groped at her shirt, ripping a button loose as his big meaty hand slithered under her good blouse and cupped her breast.

At some point, Paulie opened her eyes and met Dorothy's gaze. The other woman did not cry, did not seem shocked. A cold steel of strength ran through Dorothy; Paulie sensed it. Something she wished she had inside herself. And that's when her soul reentered her body.

Her soul. Hers. Not his. Not one single part of hers was his. So why did he grab for her so? Why did he never let go? Without taking her eyes off Dorothy, Paulie tilted her head forward, her chin resting near her chest, and with all the force and all the will she could muster she flung her head backward. The crunch of William's nose against the back of her skull was the most satisfying sound she'd heard in years. He let go of her immediately, his hands pressed against his bleeding, broken nose.

"You bitch!" he screamed, nasally.

Paulie looked back at William as he dabbed his crushed nose. William Butcher would twist and turn this scenario until it benefited him. Until both women ended up fired.

And Paulie was scrambling for more work under the threat of losing the home she had built around Willy.

"You won't get away with this! You hear me. The house—all of it! It's mine! You're mine!" He lunged at her, and it was so simple, all she had to do was step out of the way.

It seemed to happen in slow motion. He tripped on his shoelace and tumbled, stomping forward, arms flailing in an attempt to stop the fall, but it was too late. His momentum, too great. He fell into the vat of molten slurry, and just disappeared.

"I'm mine," Paulie whispered.

Dorothy stepped beside Paulie and took her hand. "Yeah, you are."

Thirteen

Truly shut the door and stood alone in the living room. The thought of going upstairs to check on her mother sent a shunt of fear spiking up her spine. But what else was there to do?

She headed to the kitchen and grabbed a glass. At the sink, she turned on the tap and let the water run cold before filling the cup. She drank, gulped really. A rivulet ran out the corner of her mouth and down her chin. She finished and swiped it from her neck, hating the feeling.

Truly refilled the glass and went upstairs. Her mother's door was cracked open. From the hall, she watched her mother sitting at her vanity. Elly spritzed her favorite perfume creating a thin, gardenia-flavored mist. She brushed her hair, which appeared glossy and longer and thicker than it had been in years. Elly had always kept her hair clipped in a tight bob, but it had grown well past her ears and lay flat against the back of her neck. Truly checked her mother's reflection; she seemed content, pleased with herself, even with smeared blood staining her chin and neck. She took a big powder puff and patted the area, setting the blood in matte crimson. She smiled. And all the while the choker ribbon necklace was clamped tight around her throat.

Truly set her hand against the door and pushed. "Mom?"

Elly's head notched to the side at the sound of Truly's voice. "Yes," she hissed.

"I brought you some water." Truly tread lightly into the room, unsure what to expect. Would her mother be reeling from trauma? Would she want Truly close? Or keep her at a distance? She'd just have to follow her mother's lead.

"That was nice of you." Elly placed the powder puff back in its container and fit the lid on top.

In the bedroom, the scent of all the floral perfumes and powders assembled thick in Truly's nose, and possibly masked another smell? Yes, a sickening tinge, which reminded Truly of turned hamburger meat, gray and slimy and rotting under the pink dye and cellophane. The underneath smell got stronger the closer Truly stepped toward her mother. Warnings, like neon signs, flashed through her mind —foul, rancid, fetid.

Though none of those warnings matched the image of her mother before her. Elly looked like the version of herself Truly had only seen in pictures. A young adult, with smooth skin that radiated something—hope, maybe. The delicate skin surrounding her eyes boasted not a single wrinkle. The sclera clear and white, the tiny red vessels and yellowish tint that Truly hadn't even noticed until it was gone, had disappeared. Elly's lips were full and glowing with a thick coat of gloss applied to them. She looked amazing, save the dried blood that coated her chin and neck.

"I ran into Phil on my way in. You want to talk about what happened with him?"

At mention of him, little wrinkles did form around Elly's pout.

"It's okay, Mom. It's not your fault. He took advantage and we can call the police right now—"

"The police!" Elly laughed and slapped her hand against the surface top of the vanity table. Glass bottles, all her tinctures and lotions and potions, rattled. A glob of red flesh among them—Phil's inner thigh, Truly realized—jiggled like gelatin. Truly's stomach flipped; she gagged, struggling to keep it together.

Elly grabbed the water and held the glass near her lips. Before taking a sip, she said, "You're such a prude." She drank, deeply, tipping the glass back and swallowing, swallowing, swallowing. The dangling cameo at her mother's neck trembled with the action. Elly slammed the cup back onto the vanity surface and belched. Truly caught another whiff of turned meat and dry-heaved.

"Jesus, Mom." She held her hand over her nose and mouth and backed away from her mother. She sat on the end of the bed, the air a little fresher. "I'm serious. What Phil did, what he claimed happened... It's assault. It's rape."

"Truly, stop right there. I am an adult, and Phil is a snack and a half." Elly's tongue, pink and slug-shaped, slipped out the side of her mouth and licked at the blood staining her face. "How you ever managed to keep him so long, I'll never know. Not with the shape you're in." Elly glanced at Truly's midsection, judgment painting her glare.

Truly had absorbed her mother's discernment her whole life. Anger flared inside of her. If Elly had consented, then what happened with Phil wasn't abuse, but it was still rape because...

"He thought you were me the whole time." Truly rose from the bed. "When *he* looked at *you*, he saw *me*," she spat.

Elly formed fists. Her cheeks flushed with more than rouge.

"Well, until he didn't," Truly continued. "I guess that's when the screaming started, huh?"

"Shut your—"

"Got a look at the real you and he ran outta here like the devil was chasin' him."

Elly's whole body went rigid, then shook. A tremor that gradually spasmed down her shoulders and spine.

Truly readied herself to run from the room.

"Gahhhhhhhhh!" her mother bellowed, then swiped her arms across the top of the vanity, sending all the bottles of god-knows-what across the room, some shattering against the wall. "You little bitch! How dare you speak to me that way!"

"What way is that, *Mom*?" Truly asked sarcastically, but she lunged backward toward the door, unsure where this confrontation was headed. The realization that she might not be safe with her own mother fell over Truly like a sheet. No not a sheet, not something to hide under, but a cape. One Truly tied around her neck and spun in, the silky fabric billowing around her in waves, because maybe her mother had never felt safe. Maybe Elly's horrifying behaviors weren't something new, but just an extension, a deepening, of all the mean and nasty things she had spewed at Truly throughout childhood.

Elly stood and paced toward her. Her new glossy features painted with a sheen of rage sweat. Tears lined her eyes. "You! You never cared about any of it! You let yourself just...*be*!" Veins bulged on her forehead and neck, underneath that damn choker necklace. A deranged kind of anger and fear played across Elly's features.

"That's enough. We can talk about this later. Lord knows, we've been spinning around it for years."

"No! How? How did you do it? How did you never care? How were you allowed to have your body just...be yours?"

"I don't understand what you're asking me, Mom."

"I was always his. He always had me." Elly let out a sad squeak. Tears streaked through the powder on her cheeks. She seemed weak and fragile, babbling about something Truly had no idea about—some deeply buried trauma. Truly wanted to comfort her; even through all the bullshit, the woman was still her mother. And she was so obviously in pain, had been for a long time. Truly reached out and grabbed her mother's fists, trying to smooth them.

"Come on. Let's get you in bed."

Elly let herself be guided to her bed and laid down. Truly snatched the afghan off the trunk at the foot of her mother's bed and spread the chevron pattern of deep periwinkle blue and teal over Elly's legs. Truly tried not to gasp or cry over how small her mother seemed. She lowered the shade and stepped out of the bedroom as Elly closed her eyes against the awful afternoon light.

Fourteen

MOSS LANDING, 1951

Paulie stood at the kitchen sink, washing dishes. She kept an ear out for Willy, which wasn't hard, the girl always chattered up a storm while she played outside. When Paulie had asked her who she talked to out there, Willy said the fairies. And Paulie refused to correct her, refused to tell her fairies weren't real. The girl had lost her father, nearly lost her home; let her keep some bit of magic.

"And who are you, kind sir?" Her daughter laughed at some response only she could hear.

Paulie smiled to herself. After the initial shock of her boss being reported missing, work had settled into new routines. Higher ups had sent someone to fill in for William and her new boss kept his hands to himself. Paulie was happy, the presence of it filling her chest in a way she hadn't noticed had been absent.

"Knock-knock!"

"Back here, Dor!" Paulie had even made a friend. One who came over for dinner and stopped by for drinks. The two of them would sit on the back porch and watch the lightning bugs illuminate the forest. And they'd talk. Talk and laugh so much, Paulie's jaw would ache. Even when things had been good with Beau, she never knew what it felt like to be as understood, as seen, as she did with Dorothy Gibson.

"Brought ya somethin'!" Dorothy said.

Paulie turned and saw the woman carried two big Mason jars filled with a honey-colored liquid. Dorothy liked to experiment with spirits—in more ways than one. The woman could whip up a stiff drink that made people sing and anxieties melt away, then she'd tell them their dead ma said hello. The woman felt safe and dangerous at the same time and Paulie loved every minute spent with her.

"What flavor?"

"Peach. Been workin' on gettin' it just right for the fair."

Paulie dried her hands and went to the cabinet. She grabbed two glasses and set them on the table.

"Ohhh!" Willy called from the yard. "That's so pretty!" she exclaimed.

Dorothy unscrewed the cap and poured two fingers of the whiskey into each cup. The women sipped.

"Oh, that's good, Dor. Folks'll come from Kentucky to get ahold of that!"

Dorothy closed her eyes and nodded. "Should make a pretty penny."

One thing the two women never talked about was what had happened that day in the plant. They'd both walked away and never whispered another word about Mr. William Butcher.

"Your girl won't have to play alone much longer."

"No, I expect not. She'll be off to school again soon."

"You mistake my meaning." Dorothy looked down at her stomach, where she'd placed her hand.

"You're?"

Dorothy nodded.

"How far along?"

"Four or five months, I think."

"That far? Do you—"

"Know the father. Yeah, some loser at the factory. I'm not telling him if that's what you mean."

"So you're going at it alone."

"You have. I can."

Paulie took another sip of the peach-flavored whiskey. It burned her tongue, in a good way. "Of course you can. You've got your pop's land and we're right down the road. I'm here for whatever you need."

"Thanks. I'll be counting on it, I'm sure."

Paulie thought of those early days of Willy's infancy with Beau away at war. The lack of sleep so debilitating she felt certain she'd make some fatal mistake. How either of them survived, she wasn't sure. Except for her mother, who'd somehow seemed to know when Paulie was near to keeling over and would show up ready to just hold Willy for a few hours while Paulie slept. She vowed to do the same for her friend—wouldn't even make her ask.

"Ouch!" Willy yelled from outside. The surprise and fear in the girl's tone spurred Paulie to immediate action. She set her drink aside and hurried to the back door. Willy stood in the yard and held her hand over her mouth. Tears streamed out of her scrunched eyes. The little girl's cheeks burned pink in anguish. A trickle of blood flowed between her small fingers.

"Willy! What is it? What happened, baby?" Paulie scooped her girl into her arms, still small enough to do so, and carried her inside. She set her on the counter, then ran some cold water over a clean dish towel. She pried Willy's hand away for her mouth, bracing herself for what she might find. Had the girl fallen? Bitten her lip? Was it her tongue? Oh god, please don't let her need stitches.

She immediately covered the injury with the wet rag, needing to staunch the flow of blood, before truly assessing the damage. Willy's crying slowed, her breath hitching every few seconds.

"It's okay. You're okay," Paulie murmured, not even sure of that truth, but needing to calm her child. She dabbed the cloth, and refolded it, noting the small patch of blood. The lip itself was fat and spongy already. After a few more quiet minutes passed, and Willy's breathing eased, Paulie stepped to the table and dipped a corner of the towel into the whiskey. "This'll sting, but it'll clean it out. Which we have to do, okay?"

Willy nodded and closed her eyes. Paulie placed her own hand in Willy's lap and told her to pinch when it hurt. Paulie swiped the alcohol across the wound and Willy whimpered, pinching the back of Paulie's hand hard.

"All done!" Paulie said. "Let me get you a clean towel and we're going to keep some cold water on this to help with the swelling."

"I'll get it," Dorothy offered. "Go ahead and get her settled."

Paulie agreed and lifted Willy off the countertop. She carried her up the stairs and into her bedroom. Paulie positioned Willy on top of the covers and took off the girl's shoes, one by one they clomped onto the braided rug under her bed. Paulie smoothed her daughter's hair back from her fore-head and asked, "Wanna tell me what happened out there?"

Willy's eyes filled with tears again. "He bit me," she said.

"What? Who bit you, darlin'?" Paulie asked.

"The Man who Lives in the Lights, Mama."

Paulie was confused. What the hell was Willy talking about? Before she could ask, a shattering of glass sounded, and Dorothy screamed. Paulie ran to the top of the stairwell.

"Dor! What is it? Are you okay?"

Dorothy appeared at the bottom of the stairs. Her face pale and shining with a sheen of sweat. "You better come down here."

Paulie swallowed, gripping the stair rail. "Why?"

"Someone's here."

"Who?"

"I-I'm not sure. Just come down here, please."

Dorothy's demeanor, her strained voice and wrinkled brow, set Paulie on edge. The linen closet door never closed completely, and Paulie inched it open farther. She brought down a shoe box from the top shelf, the weight of Beau's gun heavy in her hands. She didn't know if it was loaded, couldn't remember where Beau had kept the bullets. Surely with a child in the house, he'd hidden them elsewhere.

Paulie turned back toward Willy, who lay curled on her side, eyes wide open with fear. She put her finger to her lips, then made her way downstairs, praying Willy was smart enough to stay put.

Dorothy stood at the base of the stairs, facing the kitchen. A strange blue-green light illuminated her profile. Paulie came up behind her and took Dorothy's hand, slowly maneuvering herself in front of her pregnant friend. Near the dining table stood a figure made wholly of an oozing teal light. The light sloughed off the figure—a man—and cast showers of sparkling orbs all around the kitchen. It was...so beautiful. Paulie stepped closer, wanting the light to shine upon her. But not only that. She wanted to consume the light, swallow it all up, let it fill every part of her being.

"Mama?"

Damn. Willy had followed her. As Paulie took yet another step toward the bright figure, she remembered her daughter's injury and who she'd described had done it: *The Man who Lived in the Lights.* This figure, this man who lived in the lights, had hurt her daughter, had bit her lip. He was not someone Paulie should be drawn to, no matter how captivating the glittering orbs were that danced around him. He was a danger.

"You need to go!" she said.

He glowed brighter. Blues and greens swirling within him until she could just make out where a face might be; the deep impressions where eyes might form covered by radiating light. She thought of the gun, limp in her hand, and held it up, pointing directly at the figure's chest. He reached for it, for her, and the metal burned her hand. She dropped it, her palm seared an angry red. Light tendrils wrapped around her wrist, the heat so great Paulie cried out. As soon as her mouth opened, the figure shot forward, forcing its way down her throat. The light was substantial, more than just light; it oozed and gelled forward, pressing her gag reflex back and out of the way. As it filled her, she felt tears spring from the corners of her eyes. Overwhelmed, by the fact that she'd lost this battle, and maybe she'd lost everything.

When the figure's light leeched into her brain, its

consciousness rubbing up against hers, she saw flashes of its memory—saw herself sitting at her work desk, her slip showing as she reached for the creamer at the coffee station in the office, the can disintegrating into the salt vat, a great searing pain and burnt-orange lava. She knew who this was.

That's right… I told you, you were mine.

Fifteen

The TV blared the theme music for that awful plastic surgery show her mother liked, startling Truly awake. She fumbled for the remote, unsure of where she was or the time. Frantically, she pressed the mute button, and then she wondered how the thing had even turned on. She wiped her chin, damp with drool, and rubbed the sleep from her eyes. How long had she been out?

As the contestants' before and after shots flashed across the screen, the events of the day came back to Truly. She rubbed her temples, unsure what to do next. She'd called Susan and given her some excuse about her mother being ill, and well, that was true enough. Susan had sounded concerned and wanted to bring something over for dinner, but Truly had declined the offer, not wanting Susan to do anything more than absolutely necessary.

Besides the low hum of the TV, a kind of creeping quiet lingered about the house. It was still light outside, but barely. Through the window, Truly watched the golden-orange sunset filter through the mourning woods. A sense of dread rose up the back of her throat as she thought of the coming night, alone with her mother. Out here, only the trees would bear witness to Elly's madness, how she'd changed.

Truly checked her phone: a new text from Phil, which she deleted without reading, and a voicemail. She didn't usually listen to them, but something compelled her this time. She pressed the numbers of her passcode when prompted and listened as a nasal-sounding voice stated that the doctor had an appointment opening tomorrow morning if she wanted it. Truly cursed, unsure whether the office would still be open or if since she hadn't answered or called back, they gave the slot to someone else. She hit End, then redialed the doctor's office. When that same voice answered, Truly nearly cried with relief.

"Hi! Yes, I'm returning a message you left about an appointment for my mother."

"Name?"

"My mom's name is Elly, Eloise, Butcher."

"Okay, yes. Can you tell me why we'll be seeing Elly tomorrow?"

"Um..." How did Truly put the last few days into words? Her mother's erratic (and violent) behavior, her changing appearance, her insistence of some man living in the woods giving her instructions for grisly tasks.

"Hello?"

"Yes, sorry. I'm still here. I just—I'm worried about her."

"How so, ma'am?" the woman asked, probably annoyed to have this conversation so close to quitting time.

"Well, she's not really acting like herself. She had an episode recently where she kind of forgot where she was, seemed really confused."

"That can be normal for an aging person, to be more forgetful."

"This...isn't that. She's only in her fifties, and this seemed...extreme."

The line crackled along with the receptionist's heavy sigh. "Okay, I'll let the doctor know. And we'll see her at 10:30 tomorrow morning. Will that work?"

"Yes, I'll have her there. Thank—" The phone call ended before Truly could finish. Oh well, it didn't matter if the receptionist thought she was making something out of nothing. Truly knew better. Nothing about what her mother was experiencing could be labeled as the "normal" aging process. No, this was a full-on mental break of some sort. It didn't explain Elly's altered appearance, but Truly could only tackle one mind-altering, reality-bending thing at a time.

Now she'd have to figure out how to get Elly to go to the appointment. If Truly had to knock Elly out and drag her, the woman was going. Period. They just had to get through the rest of the night.

Truly stood and went to the kitchen for a drink. She poured herself a glass of boxed wine and called Susan again to let her know she'd need to take her mom to the doctor tomorrow.

Susan answered the phone coughing. After it subsided, she rasped out a hello.

"Hi Susan, it's Truly."

"Hi, dear. How's your mom?"

"I'm going to take her to the doctor tomorrow."

Susan snorted. "Good luck. That woman is as stubborn as they come."

Truly swallowed. "I think this might be serious though, so I'm taking her whether she likes it or not."

"Serious how?"

How did Truly answer that question honestly without sounding as if she were losing it as well? But Susan was her mother's oldest friend, she should know some truth. "She's had a couple episodes since I've been back. Not really acting like herself."

"Can you be more specific, hun?"

"Just doing things she normally wouldn't do. Seeming confused about her surroundings at times. Bursts of rage, although that's not so uncommon for her. Anyway, the nurse thinks it's just typical aging. But I definitely want to get her checked out."

"Sorry to hear that, hun. Trust your instinct though. You know your mom."

"Okay." Truly couldn't really stomach how Susan was dying of cancer and now her mother may be suffering from some equally awful fate. She let out a shuddering breath, and continued, "So I was wondering if there's anything I can help you out with tonight, or maybe super early tomorrow morning. I can come in and set everything up for you."

"Oh yeah, that'll be fine! I left a lot undone today when I closed up. So either time would work. I find myself very flexible these days." Susan cleared her throat. "The alarm passcode is just 1-2-3-4."

"Susan, that's not a password. Anyone could guess that."

"I know! But I always figured if someone really wanted to break into a greenhouse, I'd rather they not destroy anything. It's just a bunch of plants anyway. I don't ever leave the money down there. Safe's at my house. And that I use a double-barrel shotgun to protect."

"Noted," Truly said, stifling a smile over Susan's bravado. "I'll be up your way, sometime tonight or very early tomorrow, depending on how things go with Mom. Don't shoot me, okay?"

"You got it young lady. Give your mom a hug for me, okay?"

"I will," Truly lied. The very idea of hugging Elly sent an eruption of goosebumps up the back of Truly's neck. She didn't want to be near the extreme floral scent of her mother's perfume, or the rancid meat smell it covered. She shuddered at the thought of her fingers touching the dewy smoothness of her mother's cheek, let alone wrapping her in an embrace. "Bye now," she added and ended the call.

The floorboards creaked above her head. Truly listened to her mother's plodding footsteps. Her bedroom door let out a moan. She was awake.

Elly came down the steps slowly. Each footfall felt like the chiming of a grandfather clock. What could Truly expect now? Her mother as she looked as a pre-pubescent teen? She supposed it was possible. Elly's features seemed to be going back in time, un-aging, while her mind did the opposite, slogging itself deeper and deeper through some wild, impenetrable forest.

Truly braced herself for what might come next. But when Elly reached the landing at the base of the stairs, Truly recognized Elly as the old lady who had served her supper when she'd arrived a few days ago. Here was the person who'd begged to go to the flea market. Her skin had returned to its mildly sagging, wrinkly state, and Truly could've run her hands all over that beautiful aged skin. It had life; it had meaning. Maybe whatever was happening to Elly was solvable.

Elly reached out her shaking hand, and Truly hurried

toward her. Elly grasped Truly's elbow and let her daughter lead her to the couch.

"Want some tea, Mom?"

Elly parted her lips, smacking them together a bit before croaking a yes. Elly stared at the muted television, seemingly confused by the contestants all lined up in long sparkling gowns, their faces a blur—censored for the big reveal.

Truly went into the kitchen and filled the teapot. She set it on the stovetop and turned on the burner. Every few seconds she leaned back and checked on Elly, who still sat on the couch, unmoving. What had changed? How could her mother go from looking 30 to 60 in a span of a few hours? She couldn't help but think of the power plant. If the radium in the soil and groundwater could cause the big C, why not something like this? Some kind of anti-aging, mind warping illness?

She googled "radiation sickness" and found it could cause mental health symptoms—extreme nervousness and confusion. Yet it didn't explain why her mother had appeared younger for a few days and now looked like her old self, maybe a little worse. But who really knew what a slow uranium leak into the soil and groundwater could do—could change. Would they even put that on the internet?

Low exposure over a lifetime...or three? This property could be traced to her great grandmother, who'd worked at the plant for a time. Maybe there'd been some kind of generational build-up in their DNA, similar to the way trauma could be passed down.

Feeling as desperate as ever, Truly re-activated her account on FaceTalk to check some community pages. Maybe Elly wasn't the only person going through this. But a few quick searches only led to random posts about a strange man lurking around a parking lot outside a vacant storefront. Truly rolled her eyes. In Boomer FaceTalk speak, "strange man" usually translated into a Black or Brown person just going about their day. She scrolled on. There'd been a stabbing spree, called a random act of violence, at the trailer park last week. She'd have to do a deep dive to really find what she needed, and while she didn't want to feel alone, FaceTalk always had a way of making her feel lonelier than ever. She closed the app and checked on her mother again—no change.

The teapot whistled on the stove, and Truly scrambled to shut off the heat and stop the screeching. In the cabinet, she selected two mugs and found an old box of chamomile tea. The hint of a grassy meadow wafted from the box as she picked out two bags and plopped them in the hot water.

She carried the tea to her mother and warned her, "Be careful. It's hot." As if her mother couldn't see the steam floating above the cup. But Elly's gaze remained focused on the television screen—the women hugged each other, their tight, long manicured-nails gripping tanned, toned arms; their faces still blotted out—as highlight reels played on a bigger screen behind them. Their bodies were torn apart and pieced back together in soft, filtered light with sappy music playing throughout the montage.

Truly took the seat next to her mom on the couch, Elly's body see-sawing up as Truly sat. She tried to take a sip of her tea but ended up just blowing over the surface of it, the liquid too hot to even risk setting against her lips.

"I don't know how you watch this," she said.

Truly expected a smart-ass comment, her mother's usual retort, but Elly sat dazed, her eyes open and watching, but not reacting.

"Mom?" Truly set her mug on the side table, then turned toward Elly. Her knee bumped Elly's hip, and Truly watched as her mother moved like a wobbly gelatin mold. Truly clapped her hands—nothing. She knelt in front of Elly and snapped her fingers—no reaction. Truly pushed back her mother's hair from her forehead, checking for fever—none. She worried about a possible stroke and reached for her back pocket, where she usually kept her phone, but it wasn't there. She must've left it in the kitchen. As she hurried to stand, she noticed something that stopped her.

A thin dark line ran across Elly's throat, like the dirt rings her mother would scrub off Truly every summer when she was a child. Truly quickly checked the back of her mother's neck, and it was there too. She realized this was the first time she'd seen her mother not wearing that damn necklace that Truly had purchased at the flea. Was this a reaction to the velvet ribbon? Her mother had never been particularly sensitive to fabric. A stain? Possibly. A bruise? Truly edged closer to inspect the mark. She rubbed at it, hoping it would smear and that would be that. But the mark stayed the same. It seemed to be under the skin, the purplish brown of a contusion. But how could that be?

"Mom, what's this mark on your neck?"

Elly shook her head. Responsive. That was a good sign.

"What happened?"

"Nothin'" Elly's speech sounded full and warbly, as if she had marbles in her mouth.

"Did Phil do this?" A flood of anger and panic roared through her veins.

Out of nowhere, Elly cackled—completely the stereotype of an old witch in the woods. "Not him, not him," she sang. She laughed again, hooting and screeching. The tea from her mug spilled onto her hands. It had to burn, but her mother just crooned, "It was the one who came for meee! He said he'd be back!"

Truly scooted away from her mother, the coffee table pressing into her back. The TV screen flickered. She turned and all the censored bits of onscreen plastic surgery became viewable. Skin peeled away. Blood gushed. Cartilage smashed. A vacuum-like probe was shoved in and under some woman's stomach, over and over again, roaming and sucking. The body jerked and swayed with the violent movement. Staples slammed into flesh and all the while Elly laughed and laughed.

Truly launched herself off the floor and grabbed the remote. She hit the power button, and the screen went black. The room filled only with the leftover huffs of her mother's malevolent joy.

"What's wrong with you?" Truly didn't expect any kind of response. She hardly knew she'd spoken out loud.

A deranged kind of anger or fear played across Elly's features. "I'm perfect, my dear. It's you that's deficient." Her mother spoke with clarity now. "In every way you've *always* been a disappointment. The way you look. Your *attitude.*"

"What the fuck are you even talking about?" Frustration boiled at the back of Truly's throat. She and her mother had always had a relationship fraught with hurt feelings and mean words, but it had been manageable, something containable. Yet this, the way Elly stared at Truly as if she were trash, or a bug to be stomped, was new. Harsher.

Elly tried to push herself to stand but failed. She fell back onto the cushions of the couch. "You never accepted the way I loved you."

"You mean the near constant jabs about my appearance? That's your idea of love?"

"I did my best," Elly grumbled.

Truly told herself not to engage, to let it go. Her mother was having some sort of mental break and now was not the time to hash out a lifetime of pokes and prods. But she'd had enough, she just couldn't help herself. "You're just an old bitch. And if you push me away, you'll die out here alone."

Elly's mouth dropped open, then curled into a gray-toothed, uneven smile. "He's coming."

"Who? Phil?" Truly cringed. "He's *not* coming back."

Elly snorted and waved her hand as if she smelled something putrid. "Not your little boyfriend. Him. The Man who Lives in the Lights, Trulia Jane. He's coming. And he's going to make you so much better."

Sixteen

MOSS LANDING, 1951

Paulie felt her own consciousness shoved to the back of her mind, to make room for the figure made of light. She could see the kitchen around her, but it had a wavy quality to it, as if it didn't quite exist or she wasn't quite present. Almost seeming as if she viewed reality from the back of a cave or a place heavy with shadow, the deepest part of the mourning woods. She tried to move her body, bring her hands to her face, but she didn't control herself any longer. Her body was not her own, she realized.

A laugh echoed inside her head, too loud and deep to be hers, until she realized it came from her own throat.

"You stupid bitches!" Her consciousness wobbled with the steps the man took within her body. "Thought you could be rid of me?"

Dorothy came into view. She gripped the door jamb, keeping Willy behind her.

Tell her to run! Paulie thought. *Get my girl out of here.* But none of her words went to her mouth. None of her frantic cries made it to her vocal cords.

He stumbled into the chairs and Paulie sensed the pain. *A saving grace*, she thought. If she still felt what was happening to her body, maybe somewhere deep inside her she still had some control.

"Mr. Butcher, is that you?" she heard Dorothy ask.

"One and the same, whore."

Behind her eyes, Paulie watched Dorothy flinch, then flush. But what could the woman do? She had no weapon and even if she did, it was Paulie's body she'd be hurting. Not William, he was safe, tucked deeply inside her. Tendrils of himself found and explored the crevices of her mind, leaving a sparkling little slime trail as they retreated. She'd never be rid of him. And Dorothy would never hurt her. And god, what the hell would he do to Willy?

He'd already bitten her, drawn her blood. The thought of him stalking and infiltrating her beautiful daughter spurred her anger. She pushed and pushed her consciousness forward. With a herculean effort, she felt herself press back into some part of her brain.

"Mr. Butcher, please. Let me get the girl out of here," Dorothy begged.

Paulie watched as one of her own hands reached for a knife.

"Mr. Butcher! The girl is innocent! You don't have to do this! I-I'll turn myself in! They'll know it was me who watched what happened to you and didn't say nothin'!"

"It's too late for any of that."

Paulie felt the smooth wooden handle of the knife in her palm. She knew he'd kill them all. That it would be weeks before their bodies would be found brutally murdered in the woods. Her girl, her Wilamena, would never have a chance unless she ended this right here and now. Her fingers tightened around the handle of the blade, and with all her will and all her might she struggled to control her arm, then plunged the knife into her own neck.

Her old boss screamed and left her body as quickly as he'd invaded. Paulie lay on her kitchen floor, wetness pouring down the side of her neck and hair. Dorothy kneeled by her side and took her hand. Tears streamed down her friend's face.

Take care of her, Paulie thought, her gaze imploring.

Dorothy gripped Paulie's hand. "Of course. Oh, Paulie..."

"Keep...her...free," she rasped, her words barely intelligible in her own ears.

"I'm so sorry," Dorothy cried. "It wasn't supposed to be this way."

Paulie nodded, or tried to. Tears gathered at the corners of her eyes and slithered down her temples.

A ring of darkness tunneled her vision, and she looked away from her friend. She wanted to see her girl as she left. Willy stood in the doorway, confusion and fear played across her features. Her little girl's face strained as she held her emotions inside.

Paulie smiled and realized too late it probably made her look even more terrifying. She couldn't think of anything more to say, except *I love you*, but coughs racked her chest and blood bubbled up into the back of her throat. As the darkness closed in, she realized he'd even stolen her last words.

Seventeen

"Okay, you're going back to bed. Let me help you up." Truly held out her hands for her mother. She nudged the coffee table to give the two of them enough room to maneuver. "I don't know what's going on with you. But we're going to the doctor tomorrow, okay?"

Elly glared at Truly. Hate assembled in her gaze, glimmering like hope might in some other person. Elly smacked Truly's hands away and scooted herself to the edge of the couch. "Leave me alone." She struggled to stand, attempting to leverage her weight against the armrest. "You've got work to do."

"I already talked to Susan. She said I can come in whenever—"

"With him," Elly interrupted. "He's waiting for you. And I"—she finally got herself up and Truly grabbed her elbow to keep her from falling—"I need my necklace."

"You need rest."

She helped Elly maneuver to the bottom of the stairs,

then slowly, step by step, walked her up to her bedroom. The tension that had laced their conversation earlier drained away, like it always did. They had each other. No matter how toxic their relationship, family was family. And they were nearing the end of their time together. Truly felt the truth of that as sure as she felt the shadow of the mourning woods surrounding their cabin.

At the door to Elly's bedroom, a rush of cold wind caught Truly's hair. "Jesus, Mom. It's chilly in here." The early March sun wasn't enough to keep the evenings warm. Truly helped her mom into bed, then hurried to close the windows.

"Go to him when he comes for you. He'll make everything so much better." Elly tried to sit up.

"Shh." Truly tucked her covers around her mother, mimicking the way Elly used to when Truly was a child. It had always made her feel better, that tight feeling around her shoulders and ankles, even though it only lasted a moment before she'd twisted and twirled the covers around her legs. "We'll figure all of this out tomorrow. Your doctor will help."

Before shutting off the light, she looked back at her mother. She spotted the cameo dangling in her mother's grip, blew out a deep shuddering breath and let her cheeks go slack. Then she turned out the light, her mother still there, breathing softly in the dark. So frail and small yet spanning huge amounts of negative space in Truly's life.

Truly went back downstairs and stepped outside, letting the night air greet and refresh her. Mother. Mother. Mother. Since she'd arrived, that's all she'd dealt with, all she'd been concerned about. It wasn't fair. She was supposed to be hibernating, healing from a ruined relationship. Focusing on ways to make her life better, or at least how to make her life resemble what she wanted it to be.

Out by the shed, something clattered. She didn't think anything of it, maybe a tool had fallen over. She heard it again. Or an animal got inside. She focused on the area around the shed, but it was too dark now to make anything out clearly—all shadow, no light.

"Hey!" she yelled, then grimaced at the volume of her own voice, hoping she hadn't disturbed Elly. If it was a deer, her voice should have been enough to frighten them off— didn't take much, usually. But she heard no retreating foot- steps, no *shush* of hoofbeats over the mossy ground.

She thought of the neighbor's son, at large. Should she call the police? Over a noise in the dark? Please. This was the woods. If the police were called every time a sound was heard...

She went back to the kitchen and looked for a weapon— just in case. The butcherblock filled with knives was an obvious go-to, but she didn't like the idea of how close some- thing would have to be for her to actually use one. She wanted her space, room to hurt and run. She went to the closet near the front door and rustled around inside her old softball bag, bringing out her big wooden bat. It felt sure in her hands, thick and strong. She remembered the sound it would make, a crackling smack that reverberated through her arms and spine, when she hit the ball.

"You'll do," she said and went back outside. She didn't hesitate, making a beeline for the shed, even when she heard the strange *clatter-clunk* sound again. Whatever was out here, and yes, she realized it could very well be raccoons, was not all that stealthy. They didn't seem to care what noise they made, which made the raccoon theory all the more plausible. Those evil fuckers didn't care about anything.

Her eyes adjusted to the dark. She knocked the bat against the wooden platform deck of the shed and waited. The night air tickled the back of her arms. The smell and taste of char and ash wafted up from the fire pit. A great horned owl hooted in the distance. But she couldn't see beyond the inky black of the opened shed door; there, she was blind.

All around her, the ground began to pulse with a teal glow, slowly at first, but then quick like a heartbeat—*lub-dup, lub-dup, lub-dup.* Truly spun around watching, waiting, for a logical explanation to present itself. The ground below her feet glowed and pulsed as if some sort of throbbing biolu-minescence existed in the woods of southeastern Ohio. Which wasn't actually a thing. This couldn't be real. She knew of foxfire, the fungus that glowed in the dark and could usually be found on decaying wood, but this wasn't that. These lights moved and changed direction.

A glass shattered, grabbing her attention. She looked back at the house. The light in her mother's room was on. The old woman stood at her window, arms spread, gripping the curtains. A twisted contortion of pain dressed her face. She screamed and then ran away from the broken window, disappearing within the house.

Truly ran back, bat still in hand, to check on her mother. But she wasn't fast enough. Elly, still dressed in her night gown, flew through the back door and tore over the steps of the deck.

"Mom!" Truly yelled.

Elly didn't seem to hear. Her body pressed toward the woods at a speed Truly had to focus to keep up with. The groundglow moved around and between them, creating a path through the woods. Truly wasn't too far behind, and she noted her mother's bare feet and shins as litter from the woods stuck to them. She listened to Elly's labored breathing, watched the way she pumped her arms. Her mother followed the glow like a freight train, never seeming to register Truly's presence.

Truly didn't know where Elly was headed, but she was glad to have a bat, sturdy and strong and unwavering, in her hands. In the distance, cars whooshed by at high speeds, and mentally Truly kept track of the location of the highway. They trekked for a good distance, Elly never slowing or tiring, moving as if she were compelled. They came to a clearing at the edge of the woods, a road cut through the clearing, and before them was Susan's Place. The glasshouse looked magical, something right out of a fairy tale, in the moonglow. But Elly stomped over and through the grounds as if unaware of where they were or how far they'd come. The aquamarine path lit up Susan's yard. Elly followed the cut through the property.

And that's when Truly realized where they were going—the defunct nuclear plant.

As they passed Susan's house, Truly noticed the windows, like little yellow squares of sunshine. She heard the screen door screech on its hinges, and the woman's silhouette filled the doorway, a little fluffy lump following beside her. She flipped on the floodlights.

"Truly, is that you?" Susan asked.

"Yes, ma'am." Truly didn't stop, couldn't stop, even with the blue-green glowing path, she was afraid to take eyes off her mother.

"And who's ahead of you, dear?" Susan stepped onto the

stoop, shotgun on her hip. Realization painted Susan's features as she took in the shape of Truly's mother pacing forward, unseeing, moving like a puppet on a string. "Eloise?"

At the sound of her full name, Elly stopped. Her head craned back toward her oldest friend. To Truly's eyes, Elly was nearly unrecognizable. Her skin was supple and dewy with sweat, not a wrinkle in sight. Her lips were the perfect shade of dusty rose, her lashes long and dark. It was her breathing that was...off. It came out in short bursts, her nostrils flaring with each huffing breath. And her eyes, while bright and cerulean blue, held nothing behind them. A kind of blankness overtook them, if not outright hostility.

Truly adjusted her grip on the bat. If her mother was going to attack Susan, she couldn't hesitate.

"Shit, Willy warned us," Susan mumbled, then adjusted her tone and said, "You look lovely tonight, El." She stepped down the porch steps, keeping the shotgun leveled at the ground. "You'll have to let me know your secret. Lord knows I could use it." Susan playfully patted her short hair, she still had it. Elly had mentioned that Susan had elected to forgo treatment and just ride the cancer out with weed and morphine when the pain got to be too much. She was the strongest woman Truly ever knew, but even she'd become somebody's bitch in the end. Maybe there was no getting around it in this life.

Elly paced toward her friend, ignoring the brightening path. "Just a new diet I'm trying, Su." She walked around Susan, and Truly couldn't help but think of a circling predator.

"Well, it's working for ya," Susan added.

"Susan—" Truly tried to give a warning but was silenced when Susan held up her hand.

"I know, dear."

She knew? What did she know and how?

"You were never one for dieting, were ya, Susy Q?" Elly spat words like venom. "Always too good for it. Never *cared* about that kind of thing, while the rest of us starved."

"You're right. Didn't find it all that healthy," Susan explained.

Elly laughed, a deep cackle that filled the clearing. "And look where you ended up anyway. A walking skeleton, the big C eating you from the inside out."

"It was always gonna be somethin'. Can't outrun what's coming for us all, friend."

"I can. I will. He's given me that."

"Oh yeah? In exchange for what?"

Elly didn't answer. The teal path pulsed and drew Elly's attention back to it. She marched onward once more. Her arms pumped as she sped toward the line of trees and beyond that the plant.

Truly hesitated, needing to follow and make sure Elly would be okay, but wanting to stay with Susan and learn what she knew. Susan spoke first.

"You're in danger."

Truly let the bat drop to her side. "I'm aware. She's...not all there anymore."

"It's not just that. She owes a debt."

"What? To who?"

"The Man who Lives in the Lights." Susan stepped near the glowing path, but not on it, and walked toward the woods. "Keep moving, girl. I'll explain what I can."

Elly was already nearly invisible on the horizon, her pace

far outmatching their own as she barreled forward into the night.

"What the fuck is happening? You're talking like that old fairy tale is real."

"Do you see the sparkling trail before you?"

"Yes."

"Well, sometimes, and in some places, the shit in stories is real. And Moss Landing is one such place."

Truly couldn't help it. She huffed a laugh, then straightened up when she got a look at Susan's stern features. "I'm sorry, I just—You have to understand how unbelievable this all sounds."

"Sure. But this kind of danger doesn't really care if you believe in it or not. It's comin' for you, I'm afraid."

"Yeah, Mom said as much when I helped her to bed tonight."

"She did?"

Truly nodded, eyes trained on the ground, watching for gopher holes.

"Then it's as bad as I feared." Susan kept her gaze on the horizon, seemingly knowing every divot of her property, as if she were a part of the land itself. Gone was the sickly woman with a cane, needing an elbow to balance everywhere she walked. This Susan was energized, running on pure adrenaline and...spite? "I should have known he'd come after her again sometime. Willy always tried to end this, but it was never really over."

"What the fuck are you talking about?" Truly smacked the top of the bat into the damp grass with a *thud*.

"He's come to her before. Tried to get her when we were young."

"What? Who?"

"I just told you, The Man—"

"Who Lives in the Lights. Got it. But I don't understand what you mean." The pair were nearly to the end of Susan's property, but Elly was already at the tree line, her nightgown a blue speck in the distance.

"We was young then. Swimming at the quarry ponds down the way and the water just lit up, like the ground here. Your mom was entranced by it. Hell, so was I at first. It was like some kind of new magic nobody knew about. Biolumi-nescence in Ohio? Who'd've believed it?"

"It happens," Truly interrupted.

"We didn't know anything about that then. Like dummies, we swam around in it—playing, splashing, loving how it stuck to our skin when we stood up at the edge of water. Then we'd dip back under, and it would float off. After a while though, the glow began to form into somethin'. It swirled and coalesced into a form we could recognize—a man."

"The Man who Lives in the Lights."

"One and the same."

"Were you scared?"

"No, that's the thing. He doesn't look like a monster. Really he's beautiful, which is dumb of us, I know. Trustin' somethin' because it's pretty on the outside." Susan let out a little snort. "We were old enough to know better. We'd grown up on those stories 'bout him. Your grandma Willy told us over and again to watch out for some such monster. She warned of the fairies, talked as if he were their king. We laughed at her, called her crazy."

"What did he...do?" Truly tread around the question carefully.

"Walked straight up to us, trudging through the water, waving at us as if he were any other man and not one made of... well, whatever the hell shit he's made of." She gestured at the ground. It looked beautiful, a flurry of moving, sparkling glitter, only it wasn't glitter. If the story, the old rhyme, was to be considered true, some toxic residue from the nuclear plant had fused with the living cells of a man. A piece of shit man, at that."

"What happened next?" The plant was still a half mile away, but Truly needed the whole story before this man, the one controlling her mother, came for her.

"I don't think he can speak," Susan said. "Not without a body." Susan smirked, the little bit of moonlight and groundglow highlighting deep crevices along her cheeks. Mountains and valleys, generations of story come together to make her beautiful face. "He went right for Elly. I mean, who wouldn't back then? There we were standing naked as two jaybirds, and she was just...so lovely.

"He stood before her, held up his hand and she put her hand in his, like we'd never been warned. Never jumped rope to that dang song. Then they kissed. I tried to stop her, begged her to just come back up the shore with me. But she ignored me. So I went back and gathered my clothes. Started getting dressed. Tryna come up with some way to get us both away from him." Susan's mouth flattened into a line, her eyes narrowing as she remembered.

"I'd just slipped my bra straps over my shoulders when this awful, hiccupping kind of hack—*hhhch-hchsh-hchsh*—made its way to my ears. I ran right back down the shore to them, and...I'll never forget it, wish I could though. Wish I'd never seen how her mouth was stretched impossibly wide open and her eyes rolled back and her skin glowed green-blue while he just climbed inside her mouth and down her throat."

"Jesus," Truly murmured.

"Or the other one, his opposite."

"What did you do?"

"Your mom collapsed, and I picked her up. Carried her to the truck. I could see the sparkling thing inside her, through her skin, throbbing all through her body. I set her in the backseat and felt for a pulse. It was strong and her breathing was normal, so I grabbed a blanket from the trunk, placed it over her and got the hell out of there."

"Where'd you take her?"

"Back to your grandma."

"Not a hospital?" Truly asked, incredulous.

"What doctor was gonna believe what I'd seen? Plus, it always felt like your grandma had some extra knowledge. Spent her whole life learnin' the magic of the mourning woods around us."

Truly understood. She'd looked forward to getting her mom to the doctor tomorrow, but one hundred percent knew that not a single person in that office was going to be able to explain her mother's appearance. Her actions and behaviors? Maybe they'd have an answer. But there was no logical explanation for how Elly had seemed to anti-age over the course of a week. "What did Grammaw do?"

"Went straight to work. I told her everything and she helped me take Elly to her bedroom. Then she went to work in the shed. I don't know what she did out there. I was afraid to leave Elly alone. Willy came back with a hot drink and a mirror. She had me hold Elly's mouth open and poured the liquid, looked like molasses, down her throat, bit by bit. She,

Elly or that thing inside her, struggled against what we were doin', said awful things—"

"Like what?"

"Called us every awful name you can think of. Spoke on Willy's mama—Paulette. How he'd made her kill herself and how my grandmama Dorothy took over—You knew 'bout that didn't ya? Willy and Selma, my mama, were raised as sisters."

Truly nodded. She'd known something of the sort. That Willy's mama, Paulie, died when Willy was young. That a neighbor friend had raised her till she was old enough to inherit the property from her daddy's side of the family. She didn't think on it much, if at all. It was a history that seemed almost ancient to her.

"But Willy said that nasty talk just meant what she was doing was workin'. Once Elly finished the drink, Willy held the mirror in front of Elly's mouth. She kept wiping the steam of Elly's breath off the surface. And I was just doing what she told me to do, holding Elly's mouth open, not really believin' we were makin' any kind of difference. I started cryin', but Willy told me not to worry. *Evil can't help but to look upon itself, especially up close.* I'll never forget her sayin' that. And sure enough, the glowing blob appeared at the back of Elly's throat. It climbed up and out, Elly gaggin' the whole time. Willy backed up, reeling that thing out of her daughter. It seemed to take forever; she was well out of the house and in the woods before the last bit scaled its way out of her body.

"Then Elly coughed once and woke up as if nothing happened. She didn't remember a thing. And Willy, she wouldn't say a word. It was like if she spoke on it, whatever spell she cast would break and that thing would be back for her daughter. At least that's the impression I got. Elly was never really the same again. He stole somethin' from her that day, or left somethin' inside her. She was so lively, so bold, just stunning...before. Sad she never believed that 'bout herself afterward."

"So we need a mirror. And that drink recipe to help my mom."

"Oh honey," Susan paused, bit her lower lip, then added, "That ain't gonna help your mom this time. She's already gone."

How could that be? Ahead of them they could still make out her mother's wraith-like figure, her white nightgown flowing like a will-o'-the-wisp, loping through the woods. Why tell the long, convoluted story of saving her if it was hopeless now?

"What do you mean?" Truly asked. "She's right there."

Susan patted Truly's arm with that rolled-up, sympathy smile on her face.

Truly shook off the old woman's touch. "What are we even doing then?" she asked. If they couldn't save Elly, why were they tracking her?

"Well, we, women of the mourning woods, are always up for a fight," Susan said. "And if I can land a punch on that son-uvva-bitch before I die, well then, I get to cross one more thing off my bucket list."

Truly huffed an unbelieving laugh. "So this is a suicide mission."

"Might be," Susan's eyes brightened as they emerged into a clearing, a parking lot. The water towers of the defunct plant loomed ahead of them. "At least for one of us."

Eighteen

MOSS LANDING, 1968

Keep her free. Those were her mother's last words. She didn't remember much about the night her mother died by suicide in the kitchen she stood in now, but those mumbled, garbled words never left her. Willy kept them closed up, in a locket of sorts, in her mind. Whenever someone got too close to her, the locket unlatched, and she wondered if she trusted too much. She second-guessed everyone until they got tired of her bull shit and went on their way.

"Where do you want these boxes, Will?" All except for Selma and Dorothy. They'd been family from the start. Moving in to her daddy's cabin didn't have to mean the end of that; they were just down the road. She'd paced a trail to their house through the woods already.

"Set 'em down anywhere. I'll go through 'em later." The box hit the floor with a *thud* and Selma joined Willy in the kitchen.

"What're you gonna do over here all by yourself?" Selma pulled out a chair from the table and sat.

Willy shrugged. The house hadn't been emptied out after her mother had died. Most of the furniture was still covered in old sheets. There were utensils in the drawers. Everything needed a good washing, but Willy was glad she didn't have to replace much.

"I know what you're planning," Selma said.

"And what's that?" Willy asked. She felt a little outside of her body, being back in this house. She could barely focus on the conversation Selma was trying to have.

"You're gonna go after him."

"Him, who?"

"Don't play dumb. *He has but one single plight...*" Selma pulled a stanza from the jump rope chant kids started singing during recess when they were in third grade. "You think being here will make him come. You're settin' yourself up like bait."

"Your mama always thought he'd come after me, but he hasn't. Not once in all this time."

"What's time to a creature like that, Will?"

"What if my mama ended it? Paulette Butcher sacrificed herself and that's all he wanted. Or needed."

"One life?" Selma snorted. "Doubtful."

"You don't know though. We've just been living out here on a wing and a prayer for years, hoping he doesn't come back for us. Well, this is just an extension of that."

"So you're gonna lure him here, and then what?"

Willy stayed quiet because she hadn't thought this whole plan through. All she knew was that the first part of it was to return to the cabin, her home.

"Look," Selma added, "you think you're alone in this. But you're not."

"I know."

"Do you? Really?" The two shared a meaningful look until Selma broke it with a sigh. "Sometimes I think your mama cursed you with those last words."

Willy smiled; they'd had this conversation many times. How Willy had turned those words into a buffer, a boundary no one got to cross. How Selma was the only person that ever came close. Maybe Selma was right. But Willy had the means to do it, the privilege, a house given to her because it belonged to her daddy's family. So she meant to heed her mama's last words *and* find a way to make sure that thing never got ahold of another woman. Because while she had never seen him again, the skipping-rope rhyme made it clear he'd been busy throughout the years. If the stories were to be believed the Man who Lived in the Lights was neither dead, nor dormant.

Willy felt his presence sometimes. Her bottom lipped throbbed, right where he'd bit her when she was little. It meant he was close, which also meant it would only be a matter of time before he made himself plain and obvious to her.

She reassured her best friend. "Selma, I know I'm not alone."

"Then why are you insisting on being out here by yourself?"

"I'm twenty-four years old! I've got a job at the bar down the way. I should be independent."

"So it doesn't have anything to do with him?"

"Only a little." Willy held her forefinger and thumb millimeters apart and Selma rolled her eyes.

"Talk me through your plan, then. If you insist on doing this. Tell me how you think you're gonna stop him from taking ya."

"With this." Willy pulled her scrapbook from one of the moving boxes and dropped it on the table. She'd been collecting for years. Every time she went to the library, she'd sneak off to read about how to ward off evil, witchcraft, apotropaic magic...

She'd gathered information from history books and folktales. She'd listed superstitions and symbols and organized it all and still the book was only half filled. Selma flipped through the last of the empty pages.

"This is—what is this?" she asked.

"My collection."

"You making your own magic?"

"Maybe?" Willy shrugged and sat across from her friend.

"But this is all just...old wives' tales and shit. None of this is real, Will."

"How many girls went missing from 'round here last year, Sel?"

"I don't know—five."

"Five! In a town of a couple thousand. That's a lot. That's too many. I can stop him. I know I can."

"But why you? Why can't we just move away from here and live our lives? We can go to the *city*."

"No. He made a mistake when he bit me." Willy brought her book back in front of her and closed it, smoothing her hands over the cover. "Because I bite back."

Nineteen

They'd tried to turn the nuclear plant into a nature reserve, but nobody used it. Who would've figured that literally no one would want to spend a peaceful picnic day out here where they'd raped the land and spilled contaminates all over the place? Yet the historical markers and a vacant visitor's center remained. And rising 200 feet in the air, the nuclear plant's old water towers flaked with rust.

Armed with a wooden bat, a shotgun, and an elderly poodle who could barely keep up, the two women and Fluff, paced toward the towers. Truly tried to fit the pieces she'd just learned together with what she'd experienced over the last few days. It wasn't an easy explanation to accept. But since the Man who Lived in the Lights had gotten inside her mother once, maybe he'd done so again. Maybe the previous attack had made her an easy target, or maybe he'd been preying on her for years, a little bit of himself left behind, growing slowly, feeding on her for decades. A tapeworm of loathing and hate, filling Elly up, sustaining her. Maybe she would have been a completely different person had he not decided on her all those years ago.

Elly stood between the towering structures with her arms spread. Her back faced them as they walked toward her. Truly's nerves could have split her in half. Bile kept rising up her esophagus and burned the back of her throat; her breath tasted of vomit. The man who had Elly in his clutches wanted Truly next, and she'd just walked herself right up close. Like an idiot.

"Elly! It's me. Whatcha doing there, babe?" Susan broke the silence. Her voice carried around the empty lot.

Elly didn't respond.

"It's late. Let's get you on back home, El," she added.

Nothing.

Susan tried one more time. "Come on, now. You need your beauty sleep."

At the mention of beauty, Elly's body jerked. She turned toward the two women. Standing in the shadow of the two towers, she said, "I don't need a thing, silly. I'm more beautiful now than I've ever been. Thanks to him."

Elly stepped into the light and both Truly and Susan gasped. Elly did in fact appear young and pretty, but when she smiled at them her teeth were sharpened. She flicked her forked tongue in the air, tasting and searching.

"You brought *her* here. I can taste her," Elly said. Her gaze, pupils fixed and dilated, met Truly's. Her mother had merely become a puppet. Elly had sat on his lap, and he stuffed himself inside her and made her speak. At this point, all they could do was force him out of her and collect her remains.

"Yeah, I'm here." Truly stepped forward. "What're you gonna do about it?"

"Oh, I can think of many, many ways to make *you* mine," the man said. "Through me, you'll be the beauty she always wanted you to be."

The comment would've stung had Truly not heard some version of the sentiment throughout her life. She'd built up a kind of immunity toward her mother's displeasure. Sure, it niggled at her every now and then, but it didn't take full chunks out of her thighs the way it used to when she was a kid.

"You think disappointing her means something to me? She's been miserable her whole life." Truly laughed. All this *thing* wanted was to change her, mold her into something she wasn't. Just like any other dickhead she'd meet on the street. They wanted control. They wanted to enforce beauty.

And they were always, *always* terrified of being ridiculed.

"You can't break me," Truly said. "You're not as powerful as you think you are—"

"Truly!" Susan cut her off, a warning not to engage, not to assume the Man who Lived in the Lights couldn't destroy them all at a whim.

The man inside Elly made her snarl and growl like a dog feeling threatened. "You know, you're the one that brought me back to her." He made Elly stand tall, forcing her hands to move behind her neck. "With this. You see, your grandmother trapped me in here for a time." He swept Elly's hair back and lifted the clasp of the necklace. "But once she died, I was able to start moving again. Stretching the parts of myself that had been left behind. And...*oops*." As the ribbon came away from Elly's neck, a thin line, the bruise Truly had made note of earlier, became visible. Only it was no longer a bruise. A line that wept blood, slow at first, then opening like a geyser rush of crimson, black in the moonlight, coated Elly's nightgown.

"Mom," Truly reached for her mother, but Susan blocked her.

"Don't get close. Her pain is over. But his is never ending."

Truly watched, horrified, as her mother bled out. Her body crumpled to the asphalt. Her head, barely attached, slung backward grotesquely, like some kind of dummy doll.

She'd surmised her mother's end was near. But what he'd just done was nothing more than a display of violence and gore. Something to make Truly fear him and weaken her resolve, her power. Truly let the tears fall, because her mother's body lay there, destroyed and battered, but she did not back down.

Teal lights pooled around her mother and coalesced, reforming into something new, or old. Maybe even ancient. Susan sprang forward and took the necklace from Elly's death grip. She spun around and held it out for Truly.

"Take this and go," she said. When Truly didn't respond immediately, Susan grabbed her fist and pried it open, then placed the necklace, wet with gore, in Truly's hand. "Before he reforms. You need to get back to the shed, that's where we put the last of your Grammaw's things. You have to find whatever she did to put limits on him."

"I'm ready to fight him. He can't hurt me; I know it."

"You don't know that. And you can at least arm yourself. Go now!"

"O-okay," she managed. What Susan was saying made sense. If her grandmother had the power to capture this evil, then she could too. She could find what Grammaw Willy knew and use it to protect them. "Let's go." Truly fit the necklace into the pocket of her jeans and turned to run back through the woods to her grandmother's house, then realized Susan and Fluff weren't following.

She turned back toward them and grabbed the sleeve of Susan's jacket. "Susan, don't."

"We'll just slow you down."

"You won't. I can't leave you behind."

"You must, Trulia. You think I want to spend my last days rotting from the inside out? This is a far more spectacular way to go than cancer. Now, go."

Her words felt like a shove, and Truly heeded them as the Man who Lived in the Lights nearly had two legs underneath him. She ran faster than she ever had, breath puffing as she struggled to keep it under control, arms pumping. It seemed like a dream, a nightmare, where she couldn't make herself move fast enough, her whole body working to foil her plan, her need for escape. But she kept at it, even when her chest burned as much as her legs.

She crested the first set of woods at Susan's Place. Here, she slowed her pace, speed-walking over the wet grass, keeping her eyes trained on the spot across the road where she'd reenter the woods and make the final sprint home. As soon as she hit the tree line, she told herself she'd start running again, but she didn't make it that far. A deep howl, either woman or dog, maybe both, broke the quiet of the night. She raced through the rest of Susan's yard and tried not to focus on what she'd soon have to face. She thought only of planting her feet on solid ground and forcing her body through time and space with some semblance of speed.

When the lights from her house first slashed through the branches, she could have cried. But she didn't have time for that, she veered off the path and made for the shed. Her panting filled her ears alongside the thrumming of her heart, and she'd heard nothing else since the howling. She had no idea how far behind the man was, but she knew he was coming. Her grandmother had trapped him for nearly one whole lifetime; this was personal.

She stomped over the front steps to the shed and threw open the barn-like doors. She felt for the light switch and clicked it, but nothing happened. The old knob and tube wiring failed. Truly pulled out her phone. She scrolled to the flashlight icon and tapped it, then started scanning the room, but for what? She had no idea. She'd barely had time to register everything she'd just learned about her grandma, her family, herself, let alone form a plan, or know what to look for.

Truly did a quick pass of the room filled with moldy cardboard boxes. Her mother's loopy cursive penmanship identified the contents as X-mas decorations or Halloween. Truly felt Elly hadn't had a clue about Grammaw's abilities, so she opted for items she knew Willy'd had her hand in. She also knew her mother'd sold off a lot of Grammaw's stuff when she passed. Truly'd helped her run the estate sale, showing her how to use a cash app on her phone. It's how the necklace had made it off the property; she was sure of it.

She maneuvered to the back of the shed, pulling down spiderwebs and blowing dust off surfaces as she went. She figured she was looking for some kind of book: a grimoire or even a diary, detailing some way to defeat the Man who Lived in the Lights. But there was no such box labeled *Books*. It had probably been sold as well.

Her hope waning, she spotted a box labeled "Trinkets and Such" against the far wall. She could practically hear Willy's gruff, warble saying the words around her loose dentures. Truly unfolded the lid and sifted through its contents, trying very hard not to visualize the man loping through the woods, coming after her.

Truly emptied the box of an eclectic mix of miniature porcelain statues. Willy was an avid collector of Cherished Memories, weird little white children with doe-eyes and cartoonishly large heads. The grainy porcelain scraped against Truly's palms as she set each one on the counter, lining a half dozen of them up like useless little soldiers. Ash tree leaves had been used as box filler, and they crunched as Truly swiped her hand through them, searching for anything else—something helpful. But there was nothing. Truly was doomed. The Man who Lived in the Lights had surely over-powered Susan by now and would be here soon. All she could do was run, get in her car and get the fuck out of Moss Landing.

But for the first time, she didn't want to leave. Alongside the threat of losing her home for good, came the undeniable need to claim it as her own. She held the last of Willy's figurines in her hands, part of a nativity scene, a little donkey and sheep with similar facial features. She gripped it tightly, tension building, then chucked it at the wall. The piece shattered, and it felt so good.

Even better was the little slip of paper that slowly parachuted to the floor.

Truly paced toward the broken figurine, and delicately picked the paper from the shards of porcelain. A whiff of her grandmother—cigarettes and cinnamon—hit her nose, as if it had been bottled in the statue. Truly turned over the slip of paper and saw Willy's handwriting once more. A little faded and difficult to read, but the words *Healing Heart Wounds* had been etched across the top, along with a list of herbs, native plants, and milk from a beloved beast.

Her grandmother's magic was inside the statues.

She went back to the worktable and picked up another one, then checked the bottom. There was a hole she could fit her finger inside and sure enough, another slip of paper crinkled inside. She maneuvered the paper to the hole and then pinched a corner and pulled it out. This one read, *Let Love Go*. Not it. She grabbed another figure—a girl sitting alone on a stump—and stuck her finger up inside it, wishing she had a set of tweezers. When she got the paper out it read, *Banishments and Binding*.

"Bingo," Truly said to herself.

"Oh, do we have a winner?" Susan's voice croaked.

Truly sucked in her breath and spun toward the shed door as the room filled with the man's blue-green light emanating from all the cracks in Susan's body. Truly gasped at the sight of the old woman. Her mom's friend had been skeletal before, but now, she seemed barely held together at all. Truly hoped it was a testament to how hard Susan had fought against him, that maybe somehow, she was still in there fighting against him. Because otherwise Truly was alone, her only weapon a tattered slip of paper.

The man, inhabiting Susan's body, stepped forward, clumsily. Whatever had happened back at the nuclear plant, Susan wasn't as easy a fit as Elly had been. He stumbled, as if half drunk, surprised at how the body had a mind of its own, which of course it did or it had.

Truly edged away from him; the worktable pressed against her lower back. She scanned for a more deadly weapon than the note she held. A pair of gardening sheers glinted in the teal light. She placed her hand over the blades, maneuvering them into her grip. She had to get out of the shed. Being cornered in a such a small space felt too dangerous—coffin-like.

"You're braver than your mother," Susan slurred. "She could never resist me, never even tried. No, you, you're more like the older one—Wilamena. What I wouldn't have given to inhabit her, but you'll do." The creature stumbled closer to Truly, who didn't move. She wanted him close. Needed him inches from her.

She wiped her cheek with her forearm, her arm coming away wet with tears. She didn't want any of this. Hadn't wanted her mother to die. Didn't want to fight her mother's monster. Fear and doubt snatched most of her snark. All she could think was to ask him, "Why?"

Susan's mouth pulled back in a mocking sneer. "You really don't know, do you?"

She shook her head and gripped the sheers more tightly.

Susan loped forward. "My existence, my power, keeps you scared. Fear makes you mine, keeps you always within my reach."

Truly hardly made sense of what he said. She sniffed and swiped her nose, took a breath and said, "You're wrong. Fear keeps me vigilant."

The Man, wearing Susan's face, laughed and leered at her. "Oh this is so much better than I expected, my dear. *This* is submission. You will set all the things you hate about yourself before me, and I will eat them up. I can make you what you want to be in this world, Trulia. Pure. Likeable. Beautiful—"

"I don't care about that."

"Liar." He dipped his chin and smiled. "Everybody cares about—"

"Nah. That's just what *you* want me to be."

"That's certainly not what your mother thought. What the world thinks."

"Yeah, well, Mom was a little bitch." She would say anything to challenge him, to bring him closer.

He laughed again. "Oh, I like you. I'm going to love being inside you. Touching your brain. Tasting it. I bet it's spicy."

"It keeps you alive, doesn't it? Keeping us under control."

"It keeps me powerful."

"Same thing."

Truly had gotten him close enough she could smell him—fresh soil and some chemical tang, like window cleaner. All she had to do was swing, hard. For a second, she doubted her own strength, couldn't believe that puncturing someone's skin was actually something she could make herself do. Then he licked the tip of her chin.

Instinct took over. She heard the blades sliding through flesh, *shish*, felt the pressure give away, a kind of popping snap. His light oozed over her fist before he stumbled backward, gripping the garden sheers in Susan's grey, swollen hands. Truly shoved him and took off, tearing boxes down behind her as she fled.

The night air felt cool on her face as she ran through the yard. She should leave. Grab her keys—they might be in the kitchen. She was almost sure she'd left her purse there—and get the hell out of here. That would give her time, space, to figure out how to do whatever it is her grammaw had been able to do. Yes, okay. That felt like a plan.

She pounded up the steps of the deck and threw open the back door. Miraculously, her purse sat on the table, her keys next to it. She could've cried. Finally, some luck. She snatched the items and jogged through the living room, making a beeline for her car parked out front.

I thought you were nobody's bitch.

The voice stopped her forward momentum. "Grammaw?" she asked. She'd have known that crackling, cigarette-stained voice anywhere. She looked around the dark and empty room.

You run and he'll get you for sure.

How could it be? How could Truly be hearing her grandmother's voice?

Everything about the past is in the present, dear.

"What?"

I'm not as far gone as you think.

"But what am I supposed to do?"

Truly heard her grandmother's tell-tale huff of a laugh. *Fight the man. With all you've got.*

Truly dropped her purse and keys. They hit the floor with a jangling *thunk*. She pulled the slip of paper out of her pocket and read Willy's spell for Banishments and Binding. All she needed was some twine, a piece of the person, which she had—that glowing crap was still on her hands—and an iron will. She rushed to the kitchen and pulled open the junk drawer. There, partially hidden beneath a deck of cards and wrapped around a fluorescent yellow highlighter, was a wad of red yarn.

She pulled the necklace from her pocket and set it on the table, then looked for some mechanism to open the cameo. There had to be something. Wouldn't it function like a locket if it had kept the man inside all those years? But she didn't see a way to open it, couldn't even find a seam.

"Fuck it."

His blood, or oozing light, or whatever, had started to dry on her hands. She took a butter knife from the drawer and scraped some off her skin, onto the creamy profile of the women in the cameo. Carefully, when she felt as though enough of him were there, she picked up the necklace, pinching the charm between her thumb and forefinger to hold it steady. She couldn't afford to lose any of him. Then with the other hand she wound the yarn over the cameo, again and again. With each turn of yarn, she quoted her grandmother's spell, "Round and round: twine forms the boundary. Your resolve will not surpass my own. Round and round: twine holds us separate. Round and round: twine forms the boundary..."

Outside, a scream sounded. Truly turned toward the door, but kept winding, kept murmuring the words her grammaw had written. The man stumbled over the yard, his light leaking out of Susan's neck and casting a teal glow across the rough trunks of nearby trees. As Truly spoke, he fell to his hands and knees. Spasms overtook the body, and then like a banana being peeled, the Man who Lived in the Lights, tore himself free of Susan completely. In grisly strips, what was left of her mother's oldest friend lay in the grass.

"J-Jesus," Truly stammered.

She'd be happy to be rid of him, Grammaw whispered in her ear. *Keep going*.

Truly took up the chant once more, as the man, in pure light form, stood. There was no way this was going to work. All Truly had were some old words and a necklace. How could those things stop some creature apparently made out of spite and malevolent waste from the nuclear plant?

With the loss of Susan's vocal cords, he could no longer speak. Sauntering forward, he extended his arm and little bits of him, a tiny ray of light flashed outward, cutting a path through the night air, aimed directly at Truly.

No other choices, no other paths, presented themselves. No one else could save her. She was the woman of the woods now, the last guardian—nobody's bitch. And as soon as the thought came, she felt buoyed.

The others, all the ones who had come before her who had either been constrained or fought off this same monster, gathered behind her. Truly couldn't see them, but she could feel them, and a golden glow filled the small kitchen space. Her words gained a kind of weightiness. She could feel the phonemes pour over her tongue, a heaviness passing over her lips.

But his light moved, it had direction. A probe came for her, entering through the doorway. Its teal color mixing and lessoning among all the gold. Everything turned a brilliant shade of green, like the ash trees used to in spring. Seeking and searching, his light blindly pecked around the room. The kitchen was small; it would only be a matter of time before it found her and consumed her.

A barking in the distance broke Truly's concentration. Her words faltered, for only a second, but the probe of light spotted her instantly. It homed in on her location, spiraling about the room until it centered itself in front of her mouth. She remembered Susan's story, how he'd entered her mother, and she thought only to close her mouth, but then the magic would stop and he'd have her for sure. She kept on, her words keeping his light just barely at bay.

She chanted faster, creating a kind of rhythm. She could see the words, a shimmering opalescence. As they left her mouth, they pirouetted around the room, not avoiding the probe of green, but slamming into it and absorbing the light.

His luminescence grew paler and paler as she spoke. She could read her own words as they twirled and zoomed out the door, hitting the man full in the chest. With each hit a little more of his own teal light dissipated and pooled around him.

She wrapped the last length of red yarn around the necklace. What was she supposed to do now? The binding twine was at its end. It seemed to be working, but barely. She thought of Grammaw Willy, and how she'd spent her whole life out here, finding what she needed to conquer this man, gathering her own magic. It only made sense that Truly couldn't borrow it completely. She hadn't done the work. She had to come up with her own way to end this.

She set the necklace on the table. The bits of himself that were being absorbed by the cameo continued to siphon toward it.

His probing light nearly touched her lips. Fear, pure dread, over what came next flooded her whole self. And then she grabbed the tube of light, her hands smacking against it. The essence of it, slick and hard in her hands. She dug her fingernails into its flesh and shredded away chunks. Slimy bits flopped to the floor with a squelch and the charmed necklace drew them up into the cameo.

She grabbed again, this time dividing the probe in half, digging not just her fingernails but her fingers down to the second knuckle into the gleaming mass of him. Once she gained purchase, she pulled him closer, her fists under her chin. With a scream from the core of her, she tore with all her might and ripped the probe in half. The two halves lay shredded and limp in the yard, and Truly walked forward back out into the night, back out into her mourning woods.

Under the spindled branches of dead trees, Truly felt

home. She walked between the two ruined sections of the man's probe, and he stepped back, pulling the pieces with him. But it didn't matter they were already caught in the event horizon of the cameo.

A puff of some animal appeared out in the yard, behind the man. It couldn't be. Fluff? The old dog had survived? He had. Fluff barked viciously, growling and showing his teeth, performing a kind of threatening dance around the man.

The man's attention split between a vicious woman and a vicious dog, standing in a pool of his own light and another tiny trail escaped, making its way toward the necklace. He was shrinking, melting. Losing. He must have known it, which made him all the more dangerous.

The man kicked at Fluff, sending the dog flying back out toward the edge of the wood.

No! she thought. The idea of losing Fluff, who'd only just come back, sent her into a blind rage. She screamed her grammaw's words, "Your will cannot surpass my own!"

She gripped his probe again and filleted it once more. Truly felt her own energy dip. *No, not yet.* This wasn't finished. She begged her body to keep going, but the night, and all the events of the last week, weighed on her. She screamed, howled really, something primal and old erupting out of her into the night sky. She called for another adrenaline spike, just one more. She could do it with just one more push. The golden glow from the kitchen, the lineage that stood behind her, burned brighter, producing a heatwave that emanated toward her, cocooning her, bolstering her with their energy. She absorbed it, took it all in her chest and held up her arms. With one sweeping motion, she released their energy and the trees, the bark on those dead, beloved trees, began to move. In twisting, squirming patterns of milky white the larvae of the ash borer emerged. Thousands of them. Maybe millions. The night was filled with their writhing crawl out of the bark and their soft plops into the grass.

Truly swallowed nervously, not sure if the larvae were on her side or his. She looked to the ground, and the larvae encircled the pair of them and Fluff. There was nowhere to go. She either claimed her home, her body, or she lost it all to him.

One of the trees, the one most alive, which hadn't been as infected as some of the others, bent forward. Its branches scraped the ground and twisted its limbs around the man. He fought, uselessly. While he struggled against the boughs holding him, she paced forward, bypassing the probe and going straight for his face, the mouth he'd used to claim too many.

She stood before him, inches from his face. She searched for anything recognizable as human, but he had no features, only blankness. Sweat dripped from her hair. She could taste her own salt, bits of it flinging out, as she breathed heavily. As the salty drips touched his light, he recoiled.

"You've taken too much," she said to him, to the larvae, to the world. Then, staring where his eyes should be, she jammed her fist into the lower portion of his face. His light absorbed her fist, nearly up to her elbow. But she wasn't worried, this is what he'd done to all the others. Forced himself inside, getting up under the skin.

She opened her fist inside him and grabbed for whatever parts he had. The wind picked up, blowing her hair around her. But it wasn't really the wind, it was the trees, waving their branches wildly, creating their own kind of weather. When she felt she had a good hold on something hard inside him, a piece of his innards, she ripped her arm free. She opened her fist to find a blackened carapace.

The man crumpled, only held up by the tree, as the other trees swept their stems toward him and picked away more pieces like a flock of carrion birds. As the pieces came free, they streamed back toward the kitchen, back to the charm. The cameo, like a black hole, bent the man's light as soon as it entered the kitchen.

But what to do with his little beetle shell of a heart?

She carried it to the kitchen, stood over the necklace, and cracked it open like an egg. The insides, orange and gooey, dripped over the cameo which absorbed them with all the rest. Truly held the shell in her hand, and even then, after all that, she felt the urge to eat it. The instinct was wrong, didn't even come from her. He was still trying to compel her, trying to leave some part of himself behind.

She wouldn't allow it.

Truly went to a drawer and pulled out an old meat tenderizer. She'd never seen anyone use it, thought it might be left over from her great grandmother's days here in the woods. It felt heavy and substantial in her hand. The spiked edges glinted in the swirling lights. Truly placed the shell on the kitchen table and pounded it to bits she could feed to the cameo.

It worked; somehow it all worked.

After god knows how long, Truly fed the last of the piece of the man to the necklace, all the lights—teal and gold— dissipated and the wind stopped whirling and the whole of the mourning woods stilled.

She picked up the necklace, now heavy, nearly leaden in her hands.

A quiet whine captured her attention. Outside, Fluff lay

motionless on the ground. Truly ran to him, leaving the necklace behind, and fell to her knees before the dumb, sweet hero of a dog. She bent over, putting her face in the scraggly curls of hair about his neck.

"Oh Fluff, I'm sorry. Come on, boy." She avoided the singed fur along his belly. How the skin had blackened and smelled of char made her woozy. Instead, she focused on his face, pushing the fur back from his eyes that were pinched shut. He was still breathing. "Okay. Oh god. Good," she murmured. She lifted him into her arms, his body limp. Yet, he whimpered again as she carried him to the car. "Stay with me, buddy. I got you."

The vet in town had an ER. She'd take him there.

Once she got him settled in her back seat, she ran back into the house for her purse and keys. Truly didn't think twice about what she was leaving behind, solely focused on the barely living thing who'd survived this ordeal alongside her. She couldn't lose him too. Not after her mother. Not after Susan.

The wind whipped through her hair, the open driver side window rattling in its place, as she pushed the boundaries of the speed limit on 27 and created a story she'd tell the vet tech about what had happened to Fluff.

Twenty

Elly's mother, Willy, sat hunched over her worktable in the shed. The whole area was covered with pictures of missing girls and news articles about the old nuclear plant. Whenever Elly asked what she was doing, her mother snapped about *incompetent country detectives* and *the patriarchy*. Elly wasn't sure how it all fit together, but whatever compelled her mother to do this work had also kept her alone in the woods. She'd heard the whisperings from her classmates whenever they glimpsed Willy dropping her at school. *Witch.* Once she'd told her mother what they said, and Willy only said, 'You're damn right I'm a witch. How else is a woman supposed to stake claim to this world?"

Elly'd come to terms with it a while ago. Her mother was just nuts. Both exerting no guidance and too much control over Elly's life for too long. Strict one minute—especially when it came to dating—and neglectful the next—especially when it came to showing affection. Her mother only had her words, her stupid research to pass on, and Elly wanted none of it.

"Mom?"

Willy ashed her cigarette into a nearby soda can. "Yes," she rasped.

"Can I go with Susan to the dance Friday?"

"Susan? Not...what's his name?"

"His name is Jack. And no, everybody's just going in a friend group."

"That's the way it should be, El. Especially at your age. You shouldn't be worried about what boys think or do."

"Mom, you sound ancient."

"And what are you wearing to this dance?"

Elly sighed. She had two outfits: the one Willy would approve of, all sack-like and lifeless, and the miniskirt and crop-top she'd stolen from the mall last week. Elly crossed her fingers behind her back. "That dress you got me from Pennies."

Willy turned on her stool, facing Elly, and cleared her throat. "I thought you hated that dress."

"I do. But what else is there?"

Willy lit another cigarette, took a deep inhale, and pointed at her daughter. "You're lying to me now, little girl."

Elly rolled her eyes. "I'm sixteen. I barely need to ask for your permission anymore. I'll go where I want, when I want, and wear what I want."

Willy blew out a smoky breath, unmoved by Elly's declarations.

"I don't even know why I bother. Susan's mom doesn't put all these limits on her and she was your best friend."

"Was being the verb in that sentence."

"Right. You have no one, and I refuse to live my life like

you do. I'm going to the dance. I'm gonna wear what I want, even makeup. And I'm gonna make out with Jack. Because, unlike you, I care what other people think." Elly stomped away, mad at herself for even thinking she could have a normal conversation with her mother.

"Then I've failed," Willy said softly, but loud enough to stop Elly's forward momentum.

She turned around, and snapped. "Not this again! You put all these ridiculous limits on me: don't wear makeup; don't dress loose; don't date anyone, like, ever. And then you don't explain why! Why am I not supposed to do these totally normal teenage things! How does me wanting to spend time with Jack have anything to do with your parenting?"

Willy stood and gestured about her conspiracy cave. "This! This is why! Can't you see that?"

"You think I'm gonna go missing?" Elly heard the disbelief in her own voice and hoped her mother did too. How had Willy spent Elly's whole childhood worrying about something so unlikely to happen? Had there been missing girls in Moss Landing? Yes. But that happened everywhere. And besides, Elly was smart, popular, in with the good kids. She'd never put herself in a dangerous situation. But apparently, her own mother didn't feel Elly was that capable. Willy didn't trust her.

"I'm trying to protect you," Willy said. She leaned against the shed door jamb, a look of resignation on her face. "Knowing what I know, I shouldn't have—"

"Brought me into this world." Elly finished her mother's old lament. Every argument they ever had ended the same way; it never stopped feeling like a punch to the face. It knocked Elly to the proverbial ground every time, except this one. Now, she wanted to fight back. Rip her mother a new one, because god damn it, she had birthed her. She was a whole person, yet Willy preferred old, musty newspaper articles. *Fuck her*.

Elly clenched her fists and stepped closer to the shed. "I don't know what awful thing must have happened to you to make you such a bitch, but it has ruined us. I'm good. I'm smart. I'm here, and you don't see me! You absolutely have failed me, but not in the way *you* think."

Her mother flinched—finally. Maybe Elly had gotten through, made her understand.

Willy took another drag on her cigarette. She sniffed, then said, "Wait here."

Elly took a deep breath, unclenched her fists. All this over a stupid high school dance. God, she couldn't wait to get out of here. As soon as she and Susan turned eighteen, they were headed for California or New York. One of the big cities for sure. Ohio couldn't contain her.

"Take this with you." Willy reappeared on the deck of the shed. Her voice crackled over her footsteps clomping against the wood. She stepped into the grass and held out her hand to Elly.

Elly resisted the urge to roll her eyes and held out her hand. Willy dropped a muslin drawstring bag into her cupped palm. "What is it?" Elly asked.

"I can't speak of the magic I make," Willy insisted, another one of her favorite sentiments.

"Okay, Mom," Elly said, trying not to let all the sarcasm leak into her tone. She held the bag close to her nose and smelled lavender, then the piney smell of rosemary. "I'm going," she said and backed away from her mother. After a beat of silence, Elly broke eye contact and turned toward the house.

From the kitchen, she watched Willy sit in one of the chairs next to their fire pit and stare up at the blooming ash trees. Her mother looked...old.

Elly squeezed the little bag her mother had given her. The floral and pine scent bloomed around her. It had happened before. In place of words, her mother gave her trinkets. Talismans of her so-called magic.

Why is she so weird? Elly thought, then threw the pouch in the trash without even looking inside.

Twenty-One

It was mid-morning before she returned to the house amid the mourning woods. The police had already called; her cell was listed as her mother's emergency contact. A hiker had found the body—Truly was having trouble considering it her mother—at the park, and they wanted to know when they could come by and speak with her. She explained that she'd taken Susan's dog to the vet after finding him injured on the side of the road late last night, that she'd be home as soon as she knew he was in the clear...or not. They told her they'd be at her house by 10 AM.

With the absolute ruin of her kitchen and yard, it would look to a couple of homicide detectives as though she and her mother had fought—violently. Add in the shredded body of Susan near her shed, and Trulia Jane Butcher was fucked.

"Are you his owner?" a chirpy voice asked. The tech stood in the waiting room in pink scrubs with black pawprints all over them.

"N-no. I brought him in though. I'm just a neighbor."

"Well, Fluff is a fighter. Mostly, external injuries. He was lucky. You said he was on the side of the road?"

"That's where I found him, yes," Truly lied.

"Seems like he might have been hit by a car? Those were some strange burn patterns though."

"I don't know what happened. I just found him like that."

"Well, he'll need to stay with us for a few days."

"Okay." Truly turned to leave.

"Ma'am, you said you were the neighbor. Can you leave his person's name and number? We'll need to let them know what's happening here."

Truly rattled off Susan's information, feeling a wave of nausea over Susan's demise.

"I've gotta go. Something's happened." Truly felt the events of the last week pull on her body like a riptide. She needed rest before she burned out and shut down forever.

"Sure thing. Thanks for bringing him in. Between you and me, I think he'll be up and about in no time."

"Thanks." The bell above the door jangled as she left. In the parking lot, she held her keys and blew out a sigh. She could leave town—hop in her car and head south. Be on a beach by nightfall. Forget all about this nightmare with her mother. But that wasn't really her way, or at least it wasn't her way anymore.

THE SHERIFF'S JEEP WAS PARKED IN FRONT OF HER house when she pulled in. She recognized him as he stepped out of his car. Some derpy kid she'd gone to high school with, a baseball player if she remembered right.

"Hey, Kyle," she said, walking up to the house, resigned to be dragged out of here in handcuffs at any point.

"Truly, when did you get back in town?"

"I don't know, like a week ago." She couldn't believe so little time had passed. She felt like she'd aged many years since then.

"Sorry to tell ya 'bout your mom, Truly."

"Thanks? She's not really been herself lately."

"How do you mean?" he asked.

Truly plunked herself on the bench seating that ran the perimeter of the deck and started crying. As soon as the first tear ran free, Truly lost control. She wept uncontrollably. How could she ever put any of the last week into words? Who would believe her? How could she even begin to process the trauma of it?

Kyle ran back to his car. "Here ya go." He handed her a wad of scratchy fast-food napkins. "Had these in the glove compartment. They seem to procreate in there."

Truly hiccupped a laugh. "I'm sorry, I can usually keep it together."

"No need to 'pologize. It's a tragedy, Truly."

Truly wiped her eyes, blew her nose, and told Kyle about *some* of the strange things that had happened since she'd come home. She stuck to what could be easily explained by dementia or some other illness—the bunny really got his attention—and told him about the doctor's appointment she'd made.

"It was supposed to be this morning." Truly ran her teeth over her bottom lip.

"Wow, Truly. That sounds...just awful."

"And now you're here to tell me she's..." She still couldn't say it out loud.

"Yeah." Kyle wiped his forehead with a spare napkin. The March morning was warm, and he was all uniformed up, right down to a fleece-lined bomber jacket. "About that." Now it was his turn to spill it. "Based on what you're telling me, it sounds like she might have wandered off some time in the night. Run in with someone...unsavory. Where were you?" He slipped the most important question in, and Truly reconsidered his derpiness.

"At Susan's greenhouse. She offered me a job and since I had to take Mom to the doctor this morning, I told her I'd come in last night and get everything she needed done before she had to open the next day. When I was leaving, that's when I found Fluff in a ditch." She grimaced, thinking of the state he'd been in.

"Speaking of Susan, did you see her last night?"

"No," she lied. "But I need to tell her about Fluff." Truly grabbed her purse and pulled out her phone, going through the motions of sending Susan a text about what happened to Fluff. "Why?"

"Well, she didn't open the greenhouse today. Some neighbors were worried. She's got that cancer, you know?"

Truly nodded, not meeting his eyes.

"Guess I better do a wellness check." Kyle stood, acting like it was time to leave. Truly nodded, not trusting the pitch of her voice to stay solid and true. Susan's body, or what was left of it, was in her backyard. Out in the open.

"You're not leaving town, are ya?" he asked.

She shook her head, swallowed hard, nervous about what he might say next.

"Good. Answer your phone. There'll probably be a few more questions to answer. You'll need to ID the body. Plan a funeral, all that."

"Oh."

"I'm sorry, Truly. I really am." He fitted his hat back on his head. "Be careful out here." He licked his lips, seemingly pondering what to add. "We got some kind of sicko round these parts."

She huffed, smirking.

"I'm serious now. Your mom didn't just keel over, Tru. She was murdered, okay. Now, I don't want to go into all the gory details at his point, but this is legit."

"I hear you." She kept her face solemn.

"Rest up. You'll need it."

His boots smacked along the wooden planks of the deck stairs.

"Hey!" He turned back around and Truly's heart tripped over itself. This was it. He'd put it all together, somehow. Maybe the carapace of a heart she'd yanked out of the Man who Lived in the Lights still beat inside the necklace.

Lub-dub lub-dub lub-dub

Maybe Kyle could hear it.

"What're y'all doing to these trees?"

"Huh?"

"The ash trees, Tru. You're the only place around these parts where most the ash trees are blooming leaves. What're you doing to keep them bugs away?"

"Oh, I-I don't know."

"Shoot, if you figure it out let me know. I've had to fell five trees just this spring. I hate it. Makes me so mad."

"Yeah. I'll check through the shed. Maybe my mom had notes in her garden plans?"

"Cool."

She watched him drive away and heaved a sigh of relief

when all that was left of him was a puff of dust hanging above the dirt road.

Time to get to work.

She opened the front door. Arrested by the quiet, lifeless quality of the house. She stepped from room to room, afraid to disturb anything. But there was nothing out of order. The kitchen, where a whirlwind of light and battle had taken place mere hours ago, was completely restored. The back door was wide open. Yet the yard had been cleared. The branches that had snapped off, the pine needles that had rained down, were gone. Had any of it happened? She questioned herself, and her own grip on reality.

She went back to the kitchen table and found the necklace was gone.

"Fuck!" she urgently whispered. "No!" She ran her hands over the table's surface, checked the floor, and opened cabinet drawers, searching for the necklace. "It can't be gone! It can't be for nothing!" Two people were dead. Fluff was on the cusp. She'd killed the man. She was sure of it. Or at least she had been last night.

She gave up looking for it in the kitchen and ran to the front of the shed, where Susan's body had...dissipated. But the body was gone too. What was happening? Had it all been her imagination? Had she been the one losing it all along? Would her mother step out onto the back deck and light up a cigarette with some passive-aggressive comment about how she looked like fresh garbage this morning?

No.

She stepped into the shed. Everything in here was as it should be, including her grammaw's figurines. Even the one she'd shattered had been pieced back together somehow. She checked the inside and felt the little slip of paper. It was real.

Her grammaw had magic; she'd lent some of it to Truly, and Truly had called on her own. The mourning woods had attuned to her power. As she ran her palms along her grammaw's workbench she found the proof she needed. The cameo was set inside the wood, smoothed over by layers and layers of epoxy. She clicked her fingernail against it.

Trulia Butcher, and all the daughters that came after her, would keep the Man who Lived in the Lights like a trophy.

Epilogue

He'd been living in the woods behind the Butcher place for weeks, ever since the Feds came banging on his mother's door. It had been quiet, at least until the younger one showed up.

He remembered her from high school. They'd been in the same grade; partied adjacently, but never really spoke to each other. He was fine with that, had always thought of himself as a loner. He'd hated most of his classmates. All those Chads and Stacies could just go ahead and kill themselves already. Hell, if his mom hadn't been so anti-gun he'd have probably shot up that school and done it for them. Been a real wizard asshole with a manifesto and a preemptive strike against whatever shitty, boring lives they all could've had.

But he didn't.

What he wouldn't give to rewrite his story in such a way though. But no. His story. No one would understand his story. How he'd just shitposted on the internet for years. It had been a joke, until it hadn't. Those images on his computer weren't really his. He never got off looking at that shit, and he wasn't the one making it. But he was tech savvy enough to make money off it. He'd siphoned and laundered a ton of money for himself since high school, without even leaving his basement. It was gold…and then it wasn't.

Now he was homeless, except for this land.

When that sparkling, glowing glob had split into pieces in Trulia Butcher's yard last night. He'd hardly believed his eyes, but then a shard hit him in the face. Knocked him flat on his ass. He hadn't been slapped that hard since his mother figured out what he'd been doing all those hours in the dark corners of her basement.

He knew whatever hit him had attached itself. When he put his hand to his cheek, the substance felt gooey and the teal glow flooded the peripheral vision of his left eye. The piece had been smaller last night; he was sure of it. After he had been struck, he'd made his way down to a nearby creek, a tributary of the Miami, and washed his face. Last night it felt like a finger-sized gash.

By morning, his puffed cheek throbbed and burned, hot underneath his fingertips. It had to be some kind of fast-moving infection, like a computer virus or worm. He needed help and maybe some antibiotics. Only way he'd get any out here would be to break into one of the nearby homes and hope somebody hadn't completed the full ten-day regiment, which was a long shot.

He stumbled back to the creek to fill his canteen. The vision in his left eye petered out completely as the lids swelled together. He delicately patted his cheek, and the raw-muscle feel of the blob covered nearly half his face. How deep was it spreading? Could he peel it off? He had a knife strapped to his belt, had used it to skin and bone many a fish since he'd been out here. He unsheathed it and tried not to panic. If this thing was growing, overtaking his own flesh and blood, and had quadrupled in size in mere hours, he didn't have long before it covered his nose and affected his ability to breathe.

That long shot was looking like an only shot, unless he was willing to slice half his face off right here in the woods. Either way this grisly little turn of events went, he'd need a round of antibiotics.

He needed to get back to his mother.

She'd help him.

By the time he reached her back door, his mouth was covered. He desperately tried to control his breathing, but hyperventilation was a constant threat. What was happening to him? And why? His whole life seemed like such a waste. A blip of insignificance. And now he was going to have to chop off half his face or have his mommy do it, to save his life.

He knocked on the door and waited. After a few minutes, he pressed his face to the glass and cupped his hands around his good eye. The kitchen lights were off. But in the gray-green light of the surrounding forest, he could see his mother's coffee cup on the table. Her signature noir red lipstick stained the rim. He knocked again but didn't wait long. He didn't have time. The spare key should be out here somewhere. He ran his hand along the top of the doorframe, where it had been kept for literal decades, but it wasn't there now.

Stupid bitch, he thought. She must have removed it after the Feds came. Loved her son enough to leave food scraps outside for him, but not enough to have him find his way back into her home.

He swallowed hard, losing the battle with anxiety as the

edge of the glowing blob grazed his septum. He had minutes if he was lucky, and nothing about this seemed lucky.

He looked around his mother's stoop. Potted plants lined the edge of each step. He kicked one. The terra cotta cracked on impact and tipped into the grass. A watermark stained the cement where the planter had been, but there was no key. He could just punch through the glass of the back door. He threw his backpack off his shoulders and stripped his jacket off. He wrapped it around his fist and stomped back up the stairs. He readied his stance and cocked his arm back.

"Hello?" His mother, pink gardening gloves stained with soil, wandered around the side of the house. "Is someone—Oh!" She stepped back and held her hands up. "What the—"

He put his arm down. He couldn't speak. Couldn't even explain who he was. Impotent again. Unable to do the damn thing. Couldn't even save himself.

The glob reached his nostrils now. It would only take a minute, maybe three, for it to be over. And he'd just wink out. He went down the stairs again and lay in the grass. The ash trees of his family's property were spindled and dead and poked the gray sky above.

His mother's face came into view. For a moment he was thankful, she was the only person he'd want to see before his wasted life ended. She recognized him; he could see it in her eyes.

"Oh, my baby, what's happened to you?"

He shook his head, unknowing what this was or why it was overtaking him.

His vision blinked out, clouded over by spots of black and that teal, oozing light. His mother shook him, called his name over and over, tried to pull the covering off his face. She only succeeded in scratching what skin he had left. He lay there bleeding, suffocating. Panic rose in his chest, and anger. How could it all amount to this? To nothing. As his heartbeat pounded frantically in his chest a coolness spread throughout his body.

Maybe it wasn't such a bad thing to die. He let go, letting the oozing light take over. And take it did. He found himself cocooned by it. He watched his hand reach out and grip his mother by the throat. The surprise in her eyes thrilled him. He'd seen it before in women and girls, but not up close like this.

Not so close he could smell the fear in her breath.

He needed desperately to taste it. His other hand gripped her cheek and forced her mouth open and that's how he tucked himself back inside his mother.

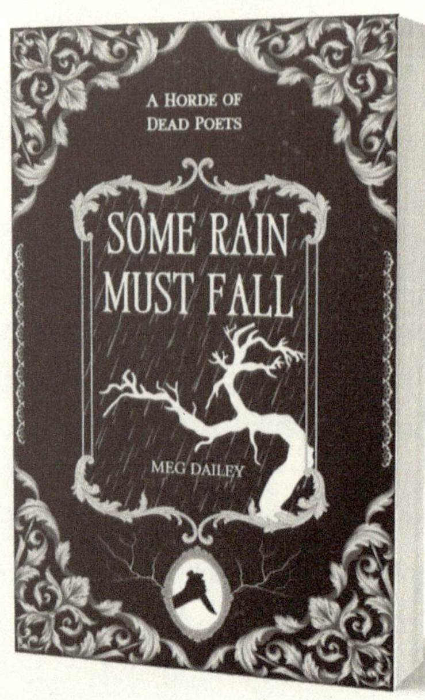

Preview the next book in
A HORDE OF DEAD POETS
collection!

AVAILABLE NOW

One

The next morning, I wake groggy as hell and with an ache in my abdomen but not much else to show for my wild night out. It's probably for the best that I didn't dream. My dreams can get vivid, and if I'm particularly tired, I'm prone to sleep paralysis. Thankfully, I haven't had an episode in the six months I've been cursed. I don't know what I'd do if I had to face the shadow monster of my nightmares while tired *and* paralyzed.

I drag myself out of bed one limb at a time, arms flopping over my body to propel my torso up as my feet reluctantly meet the floor. I take a moment to wiggle my bare toes in the soft rug. It's almost enough to lure me back into bed, the reminder of soft comfort. But alas. If I'm not dead, I have to go to work.

Shouldn't have tried to die on a Sunday, I chide myself. *Oh well.*

As if I hadn't tried to escape it, my schedule runs through my head: check in; set up my crystal ball and tarot cards on the table at the back of the shop; settle behind the curtain that pretends at privacy while I conjure the dead for the living to chat with.

I've talked to Miss Tess about adding an actual room, a truly closed off space for me to do my work. I've even made the argument that it would be better for the ambiance. After all, a medium is only as good as the aesthetics she calls on—because the ghosts she calls on can't always be bothered. Miss Tess—correctly—made the counterargument that what I really wanted was a place to hide out from wandering customers, lest I must speak to the living more than necessary. And then she said no and shooed me back to my curtain.

Curtains may be temporary, but forced customer service lasts forever.

My mouth tastes of mud, so I brush my teeth and tongue twice. My hair is matted, leaves still stuck behind my ears, and I rush through a quick shower, too hot and too short, and watch the evidence of my misadventure in the woods swirl down the drain.

As I step out of the shower, I catch a glimpse of myself in the mirror and nearly fall backward into the tub.

Fuck, I look spooky. Which is normally part of the ambiance—black hair long enough to drape dramatically into my eyes and skin so pale I could pass for a ghost myself half the time, really makes for a good show in the right lighting—but Christ alive, could I not jump scare myself please?

My not-quite-death has me off-kilter.

Once I've settled from the scare of seeing myself, I spot the shadow in the corner of the room, watching from behind the wall that hides my toilet. It shifts slightly, and I flinch again. I try to ignore it as I do my makeup, but as soon as I lean in and bring the eyeliner pencil to my eye, the shadow darts toward me, and the glass of the mirror cracks. I jump back half a second before the shadow makes contact, and glittering glass rains down into the sink and vanity with a sound like bells, if bells were tailor-made to rip you to shreds.

Well. Fuck.

I step as carefully as I can around the sharp, shining obstacle course, then dust my feet off once I'm clear, just in case. There's no time to clean that mess up now, but luckily I live alone, so it won't be a danger to anyone else until I get back.

I shuffle back to my room to quickly do my eyeliner in the small plastic mirror on my dresser and pull on my outfit for the day. My dark socks and long black dress stick to me in the places I don't have time to dry, and my hair—that'll get taken care of on the ride. Assuming it isn't raining still.

Halfway through lacing up one boot, I glance out the window.

Yeah, it's still raining.

It's always fucking raining.

Downstairs, I snatch my cross-shoulder work bag off the couch a little too quickly, and my tarot deck slips out through the battered zipper along the top, spilling across the couch and floor, a prophetic game of 78 pickup.

"Wow, rude," I scold the cards as if they did it on purpose. As I scoop them up and pack them more securely into a pocket inside the bag, I wonder who will be getting the influence of my family's twenty-year-old couch in their reading today.

I could leave most of this stuff at work if I wanted, but I've always been a little protective of my gear—my cards, my crystal ball, my favorite lavender-scented incense sticks and the gryphon-shaped burner I set them in. Even the non-magic pieces are special to me, especially the Zippo Callie got me for my birthday last year: it's silver and has stars engraved on every side. Very good for the ambiance. I grab a poncho and throw it on over the bag, which hangs in a blob right above my hip.

Outside, it's drizzling more than full-on raining, which is a relief, at least until I start moving.

My bike leans against the house, the pale blue of its paint just about matching the faded blue of the siding. It would almost blend right into the wall if not for the dark slashes of the rubber handles and the darker circles denoting the tires. I've never had a car of my own. I can drive—when the house was still my parents', they'd send me out on errands occasionally in their car—but the few trips I take these days that require more than a bike can be done in Aaron's car. Plus, cars cost money, which I can't say I have in spades right now.

As I'm wheeling the bike away from the house, movement in the trees catches my eye, and I whirl, the handles nearly sliding right out of my hands.

A squirrel darts up the tree, away from me.

"Oh, fuck off," I mutter, shaking myself.

I'd say I'm just being afraid of my own shadow, but I'm not sure how literal of a description that is. I still don't know what's following me, but I wish more than anything that it would stop.

If it was a ghost, it would be a piece of cake for me to get rid of it. As a medium—the ghosts-only kind of necromancer —poking through the Veil to pull souls through or push them back is my specialty. I've been doing it since I was ten. I can tell when it's a soul refusing to go—the three up in my attic, for example, won't budge an inch. They were there long before me, and I wouldn't be surprised if they were there long after me too.

But this shadow thing? It's not like them. At least those three I can feel, the presence of a soul like a cold spot in a warm bath. I've only ever felt two things when I tried to touch the shadow: hot, searing pain or nothing at all.

I'm not sure which is worse, to be honest. Nothing should feel like nothing.

I pedal away as fast as I can make my tires go in the muck, hoping I don't see anyone else on the way into town. That would be my luck, to be tired, wet, *and* late because I got accosted on the one road to and from my house.

Today, though, the road seems to be blessedly empty—probably because it is cursedly muddy as fuck. My treads eat up the distance anyway, so, small blessings.

It's a relief to finally hit the paved road that leads into town. Nothing beats the smell of petrichor off a road on a warm day. Today is chilly, all of last night's heavy heat having dissipated, but the smell tickles my nose anyway, teasing warmer weather.

It feels like we haven't seen the sun in weeks. Months, maybe. Summer showers bring May flowers, but cold fall showers just bring gloom.

At least I'll be able to use that gloom at work.

Ambiance.

ENJOY THESE NOVELLAS IN ANY ORDER!

A HORDE OF DEAD POETS
A BETTER GRAVE THAN THIS
JESSICA CRANBERRY

A HORDE OF DEAD POETS
SOME RAIN MUST FALL
MEG DAILEY

A HORDE OF DEAD POETS
SUCH GOOD BONES
LENN WOOLSTON

A HORDE OF DEAD POETS
IN THE HAUNTS OF GOBLIN MEN
CANDACE ROBINSON
S.G.D. SINGH

A HORDE OF DEAD POETS
DEATH'S MAIDEN
ELLE BEAUMONT

A HORDE OF DEAD POETS
DESCENDANTS OF THE BIG HOUSE
VONZALE LEWIS

A HORDE OF DEAD POETS

Acknowledgments

Thank you, readers. You invest time and money and brainspace, trusting in an adventure of someone else's making. I hope this one was worth it.

To C. Vonzale Lewis, thank you for always pushing me to go deeper and for your endless support and vision. Percy's Heart Press wouldn't be here, if you hadn't called and assured me we could do this.

To Elle Beaumont, thank you for your boundless energy and generosity in most things, but especially regarding all things publishing.

To my husband, Josh, and final-final-final draft reader, thank you for always supporting my endeavors and all the kind ways you tell me I'm being overly wordy and confusing.

While I lose the courage to right on the reg, I'm lucky enough to love people who believe in me, especially my two favorites. Tanner and Owen, thank you for always knowing your mom can be who she wants.

About Jessica Cranberry

Jessica Cranberry lives in the Sierra Nevada foothills with her family and spends days striking a balance between parenthood, teaching, and writing–mostly suspense novels and an eclectic mix of short stories. When she's not doing those things, she's reading, attempting to garden, or hiking around town. She's an okay baker, and has been known to paint on occasion.

jessicacranberry.com

 instagram.com/itwasjess

 bsky.app/profile/itwasjess.bsky.social

Also by Jessica Cranberry

Hazel & Maeve: The Campus Mysteries

In the Trap

Amid the Haze

Anthologies

Emporium of Superstition

The Darkest Lullaby